D0031224

THE LOCKED GARDEN

ALSO BY GLORIA WHELAN

After the Train

Parade of Shadows

Summer of the War

The Turning

Listening for Lions

Burying the Sun

Chu Ju's House

The Impossible Journey

Fruitlands

Angel on the Square

Homeless Bird

Miranda's Last Stand

Indian School

THE ISLAND TRILOGY:

Once on This Island

Farewell to the Island

Return to the Island

GLORIA WHELAN

The
LOCKED
GARDEN

HARPERCOLLINS*PUBLISHERS*

The Locked Garden
Copyright © 2009 by Gloria Whelan
All rights reserved. Printed in the United States of America.
No part of this book may be used or reproduced in any manner whatsoever without written permission except in the case of brief quotations embodied in critical
articles and reviews. For information address HarperCollins Children's Books, a
division of HarperCollins Publishers, 1350 Avenue of the Americas, New York, NY
10019.

www.harperchildrens.com

Library of Congress Cataloging-in-Publication Data
Whelan, Gloria.
  The locked garden / Gloria Whelan. — 1st ed.
    p. cm.
  Summary: After their mother dies of typhoid, Verna and her younger sister,
Carlie, move with their father (a psychiatrist) and stern Aunt Maude to an asylum
for the mentally ill in early-twentieth-century Michigan, where new ideas about
the treatment of mental illness are being proposed but old prejudices still hold
sway.
  ISBN 978-0-06-079094-3 (trade bdg.)
  [1. Psychiatric hospitals—Fiction. 2. Mental illness—Fiction. 3. Single-parent
families—Fiction. 4. Sisters—Fiction. 5. Aunts—Fiction. 6. Family life—
Michigan—Fiction. 7. Michigan—History—20th century—Fiction.] I. Title.
PZ7.W5718 Lo 2009   2008024637
[Fic]—dc22   CIP
                                                                     AC

09 10 11 12 13   CG/RRDB   10 9 8 7 6 5 4 3 2 1
❖
First Edition

To all those who worked
to preserve Building 50
of the Traverse City State Hospital,
and to find for it a new and different life

ONE

We were standing on the front porch as our belongings were carried from the wagon into our new home. Just down the road was the asylum. It was the largest building I had ever seen, spreading across acres of ground and towering over the flat, empty countryside. Its two wings stretched toward you like arms. "Welcoming arms," Papa said. I wasn't sure.

The chimneys were shaped like turrets. "It's a castle," Carlie said. Carlie was my six-year-old sister, Caroline. Carlie thought the barred windows were to keep in a princess.

"The asylum is for sick people," Papa explained to Carlie. "It is a hospital for people who have a sickness of the mind or the spirit. They come here to get better.

Asylum is from the Greek word ασυλον, meaning 'sanctuary, a place of shelter.'" Where words were concerned, Papa never missed a chance for a lesson.

Aunt Maude said, "More like a dungeon if you ask me." Aunt Maude saw only the gloomy side of things. Happiness made her miserable, and joy to Aunt Maude was a sin.

"How can they be happy in there, Papa?" I asked. When I was sad, I liked a good run down a hill.

Papa put an arm around me. "The patients know that they are here to be helped by people like me." Papa was a well-known psychiatrist. He had written learned papers that had been published in the *American Journal of Insanity.*

Carlie was still seeing the asylum as a castle. "I think they are waiting for a prince to come and set them free."

Aunt Maude said, "That's nonsense, Caroline. I'm sure it isn't proper for us to be standing out here on the porch for everyone to see. Come inside, girls, and help me put things away."

Our furniture looked uncomfortable in its strange setting, like a person wearing someone else's clothes, but our little home was very pleasant. Some houses shut you out the minute you walk through the door. No matter how long you live there, you are always a stranger. This house was friendly and welcoming. There was a fireplace in every room to keep us warm against the northern Michigan winter and a sun porch for the summer. There was a pantry, a kitchen, a parlor, a study, and a bedroom downstairs for Papa and one for Aunt Maude. Carlie and I would share a room up a narrow stairway. Our room was tucked under a sloping roof and had a small window.

Though I thought our new house very pleasant, I was sorry to leave my old home in the city, worried that I might leave behind my happy memories of Mama. I hated having Aunt Maude mix her memories of Mama in with mine, for they all seemed to be of Mama's illness and death.

While Carlie hunted for her dolls, Papa looked for his books, and I checked to be sure my journal was wrapped inside my long underwear, where I had hidden it. Aunt Maude reached into a box and held up a dress of Mama's. It was white cotton printed with blue flowers, and I remember Mama wearing it summer afternoons. When we gave her things to the church, for poor people, Aunt Maude had insisted on keeping some of them. "I remember when your dear mother wore this," she said. "How young and happy she looked, and now she is gone."

At these sad words Carlie burst into tears, and Papa

hurried off to the study, shutting the door behind him.

Aunt Maude was my mother's older sister. "Dear, dependable Maude," Mama used to say. After Mama's death from typhoid, Aunt Maude came to live with us. At the sad time of Mama's death it was natural that Aunt Maude should have black dresses and mournful looks. But two years had passed. Carlie had become used to thinking of Mama in Heaven, where she was sure Mama watched over us and ate suppers that were all desserts. As for me, I had used up my tears and was looking about me and even smiling. Those smiles were ever the occasion of Aunt Maude's chiding me. As her fingers would trouble the brooch that contained a tiny wreath woven of Mama's hair, Aunt Maude would say, "How brave you are, Verna, to find a smile in spite of your terrible loss. I wonder how you find the strength to put your dear mama out of your mind, but you can be sure I, for one, will never forget her." Though I had tried to climb out of my sorrow, after such words as that I would fall back and have to begin my struggle all over again.

I had hoped in our new home things would be more cheerful, but here was Carlie in tears and Papa behind a closed door. I blamed Aunt Maude and couldn't keep myself from saying, "You have made Carlie cry."

"Nonsense," Aunt Maude said. "You are very rude,

Verna. Caroline is just thinking of your mama. Come to Aunt Maude, my dear." She drew Carlie to her and soothed her with a peppermint drop. It was very wicked of me, but sometimes I thought Aunt Maude made Carlie cry just so she could comfort her.

I could see the asylum through the window, and I wondered if people there felt as miserable as I did, for nothing was turning out as I hoped. When Papa was offered the opportunity to come to the asylum, he asked Carlie and me if we minded moving to a new home. "These last two years have been unhappy ones," he said. "Let us make a new start."

Carlie said she would go if she could bring her clothespin dolls and her stuffed rabbit, Promise. Promise got its name when Carlie begged for a pet and Papa gave her a stuffed rabbit, promising that when she was old enough to care for it, she might have a real one. For myself, I thought more about what would remain than what I would take. I hoped that by moving, we might leave Aunt Maude behind, but when I asked, "When will Aunt Maude go back to her own home?" Papa looked startled.

"There will be no going back to her own home, Verna. She will of course go with us. You haven't forgotten that Aunt Maude has rented out her home."

So I knew there would be no new start.

Aunt Maude had been against the move. In a voice that whined and scolded all at once, she asked Papa, "Edward, how can you leave the home that you and my poor sister shared? How will you keep her memory in strange surroundings?"

Papa said, "I need no house to remind me of Isabel. She will be with me wherever I go, but this is an opportunity I can't pass by, Maude. The asylum is as fine a hospital as any in the land. Dr. Thurston, its director, is skeptical of my theories, but he is an open-minded man and will allow me to pursue my research. It is an embarrassment that in this year of 1900, when we have an airship that can sail through the skies, we can think of no better way to cure diseases of the mind than to shut people up. I am convinced that one day we will find a remedy for such illness in our medicine chest."

Now we were in our new home, but everything was the same. A hundred times I had resolved to be nicer to Aunt Maude in hopes she would be nicer to me. I knew she would never like me as much as she liked Carlie, but maybe I could get her to like me a little. I lifted a box marked "china" onto the dining room table. "Would you like me to unpack these dishes, Aunt Maude?"

"Put that box down, Verna. That is your mother's

best china, handed down from our own mother. No one handles those dishes except me."

I thought Aunt Maude's heart must be like a tiny house with only a very little room inside, just enough for Carlie but not enough for me. When I was younger, I used to play a game with Carlie. We would go for a walk and then pretend we were lost, wandering up and down the street, looking for our house, making believe it wasn't there. We would frighten ourselves and cry until one of us tired of the game and we ran home. I felt lost now, but this time it was no game, and there was no familiar home to run to.

TWO

On the first night in our new room we discovered that there was a poplar tree outside our window. Its noisy leaves kept Carlie awake. "Why is the tree angry?" she asked, and climbed into bed with me.

But the next morning was bright and fine, and the soft chatter of the leaves seemed friendly, not angry. We had moved to the asylum in June, after our school term was over, so we were soon outside in the sunny weather. Aunt Maude worried when we were out of the house. She appealed to Papa. "Surely it is dangerous for the girls to wander around the grounds of the asylum, Edward. A patient might do them harm."

Papa was reading a journal. I knew he hated to be talked at when reading. Any answer at such a time would be quick, cross work. He looked up and said, "Maude, that is nonsense. They are perfectly safe here, and fresh air is good for the girls. I would not be surprised to find a little healthy activity to be of benefit to you as well. You would not have so many great concerns over small matters." With that Papa escaped to his office to work on his book.

After Mama died, he began to write a book about his ideas for curing people in asylums. It was to be called *The Closed Mind*. Papa would shut himself into his study and work away night after night, so Carlie and I called the book *The Closed Door*. I believe that when Papa is writing, he doesn't think so much about Mama. Words are Papa's medicine. When Mama was alive, Papa used to spend time with us in the evenings. He told us stories about when he was a boy. His papa worked as a printer for a newspaper. Papa would help his father make words with hundreds of pieces of wooden type. He grew to love words. He gives Carlie and me a penny for every new word we bring to him.

Now Papa was back behind the closed door, and Carlie and I were left on our own. But there was so much to explore that Carlie and I didn't mind. Since we had always lived in a city, the countryside around the asylum appeared vast and empty, but the more we explored, the faster it filled up. The asylum stood in the midst of trees and shrubs. Carlie and I could hide from Aunt Maude in the tangles of shrubs and up in the trees. In the city it had been hard to disappear, because everything belonged to someone who didn't want you there. But here we could hide for hours.

Many of the trees were newly planted, so the asylum appeared to stretch even higher over everything. It was a small kingdom. Gathered about the large building was a little cluster of houses, like children about their father. Beyond the asylum were its barns and silos and fields. The word *silo* got me a penny from Papa. At the far edge of the fields was a small lake, but we had been warned against going there.

I knew little of trees and plants. Among the familiar birches and maples we saw many strangers with oddly shaped trunks and puzzling leaves. There were flower beds everywhere: cheerful red geraniums; flocks of daisies; peonies whose pink petals crawled with ants, spoiling their prettiness. Though I warned Carlie that it was forbidden, she couldn't resist snatching at a flower here or there, so she always arrived home clutching a ragged bouquet.

One day, we discovered a garden tucked away behind the asylum, with a high iron fence all around it and a locked gate. We pressed our faces against the bars of the fence, feeling their cold hardness on our skin. Inside was a fountain making a faint rippling sound as water spilled over into a stone basin. I wondered who was allowed into the garden and how the flowers and trees felt shut up all by themselves.

Often in our explorations we came upon patients strolling about the grounds or making their way to the barns and fields where they worked. At first we were wary of them, keeping out of their way, but we soon saw that they were much like anyone else. Carlie, who could not let strangers pass by without making their acquaintance, was soon calling many of the patients by name. There were nearly a thousand, some of whom, Papa said, were not well enough to walk freely outside. When Carlie and I looked up, we saw faces at the barred windows, kings and queens imprisoned in their castle.

We were assigned a maid, Eleanor Miller, to care for us. When Aunt Maude learned that Eleanor was a patient from the asylum, she was horrified. "A mad-woman in our house! Never."

Papa explained, "It is the custom, Maude, for patients who are making a recovery to assume some work respon-sibilities. In addition to helping to pay for their costs, they gain experience that will assist them in finding employment when they are discharged from the asylum. Work is natural to man and is an important part of the patients' treatment."

Aunt Maude was not calmed. "We will awaken with our throats slit."

A little shiver went through me, but Papa only smiled and said, "If our throats are slit, I think we will not bother to awaken. I have seen Eleanor's history. She has been suffering depression and is coming out of it nicely. She wouldn't hurt a fly."

Eleanor arrived as Carlie and I were finishing breakfast. Papa was already at the hospital. Eleanor did not look as though she could do anyone harm. She was young and slim, even a little bony. Her hair was so fair that it was nearly silver, and so fine that though Eleanor had knotted it and stuck it in place with many pins, strands and wisps escaped, making her head look surrounded with a silver halo. Her best feature was her eyes, bright blue, under pale lashes. Her worst feature was her hands, red and chafed.

When she saw me looking at them, she hid them behind her back. "Farm girl hands," she said. "I'm used to scrubbing and cleaning." She turned to Aunt Maude. "I'm not afraid of work. Just tell me what I must do."

"There will be plenty to do," Aunt Maude said. "I

only hope you know how to handle nice things. I don't suppose you were used to them at the farm."

"My mama has a bowl, all cut glass," Eleanor said. "With the sun on it, it shines like a diamond."

"We don't have time to listen to what your mother may have," Aunt Maude said. "The kitchen floor needs a good scrubbing."

Eleanor hurried to fill a pail and went to work, humming to herself until Aunt Maude said, "There is no need to make that noise," but after watching how hard and cheerfully Eleanor worked all day, Aunt Maude had to admit to Papa that evening that Eleanor "had possibilities."

Much to Aunt Maude's irritation, Carlie took to following Eleanor about all day like a little puppy. When Carlie learned that she could speak German, she begged Eleanor for German words. Eleanor taught her *Haus*, *Brot*, *Schwester* for "house," "bread," and "sister." Carlie ran to Papa with the words and got three pennies.

At first I didn't pay much attention to Eleanor, but one day we both were out in the backyard, Eleanor beating dust out of the rugs and I sitting in the shade of an apple tree, reading a book. I put my book down and asked Eleanor, "Do you like coming here every day instead of being at the asylum?" I was curious about Eleanor. Even though she was a patient, she didn't seem all that different from me.

"Oh, yes. It's dull there without much to do, and it's bad for my melancholia when I'm shut up."

"What does *melancholia* mean?" It sounded more like something you ate than a disease. I repeated the word to myself, thinking I could get a penny from Papa for it.

"The doctor says it's a kind of sadness," Eleanor said. "It's like a tune that stays in your head, and you can't get rid of it."

When I asked her why she was sad, Eleanor only shook her head. "I keep my sadness to myself," she said. "There is no need to make you sad as well."

I knew exactly what she meant, for Mama's death was like that for me. When Carlie thought of Mama and missed her, she cried and let everyone know what she was feeling, but when I thought of Mama, I just wilted like a flower kept out of water and didn't let anyone know how I felt. I decided Eleanor and I were alike, and after that, I knew I had someone I could talk with as I used to talk with Mama—and couldn't talk with Aunt Maude.

The first chance I had to be alone with Papa, I begged him, "Send Aunt Maude away, Papa. I'm twelve now and I can take care of Carlie, and Eleanor will take care of the house."

"Verna, I'm ashamed of you. You should be grateful to your aunt for all she is doing for us. Of course I won't send her away. Eleanor is not entirely well and can't manage both you girls and the house."

"Not entirely well," Papa had said. But Eleanor, who was cheerful and, in spite of Aunt Maude's complaints, went about her work singing to herself, did not seem ill to me. I thought how pleasant it would be to have Eleanor instead of Aunt Maude to care for us. When I saw that Papa would not send Aunt Maude away, I resolved to find a way to make her leave, giving no thought to what my scheming might mean for Eleanor or Aunt Maude. I thought only of what I wanted.

We were welcomed to our new home by the wives of the other asylum doctors, who came wearing hats like platters heaped with flowers and feathers. They brought covered dishes of scalloped potatoes, roast chicken, apple coffee cake, and molasses cookies. Mrs. Thurston, the wife of the hospital's superintendent, brought little frosted cakes, each one with a real sugared violet on top. I thought them the most beautiful cakes I had ever seen, and Carlie asked if they were fairy food, but Aunt Maude declared them frivolous. (Later, when the women were gone, I looked up the meaning of the word so I could take it to Papa for a penny. The dictionary said *frivolous* meant "lacking serious purpose." I did not see why everything must be put to a serious use. I reminded Aunt Maude of the Bible's lilies of the field, which "toil not, neither do they spin" and she said I was being "impious," which got me another penny from Papa.)

Aunt Maude had me put on my best dress and pass the refreshments. I heard her confide her fears to the women. "How can an asylum be a suitable place to bring up children?" Though Eleanor was nearby in the kitchen, taking care of Carlie, Aunt Maude did not bother to lower her voice but asked, as she had asked Papa in different words, "Are not the patients dangerous?"

"Oh, never in the world," Mrs. Thurston said. "There is nothing of that kind here. Of course there are disturbed patients in the back wards, but they don't go about. You could not find a more pleasant spot than the asylum to raise children: fresh milk and butter from the asylum's own cows, fresh vegetables from its gardens, help in the house, and a congenial society." She smiled. "Of course we are isolated here, and in any close society there will be little quarrels and gossip, but I would be surprised if the saints in Heaven itself didn't have their little differences."

Aunt Maude frowned. She did not like jokes about holy things.

I was about to hear some of the gossip Mrs. Thurston

had mentioned. Mrs. Larter, who had a hat with what looked like a small dead bird resting on it, said, "Last year there was a very unpleasant episode when a staff member became too friendly with one of the patients. The staff member had to be let go because—"

Mrs. Thurston's glance fell upon me. She interrupted Mrs. Larter, saying to us, "Unfortunately, Verna, just now the doctors' families are an older group, and there are no children your age here, but you and your sister will have each other and will make friends when school starts this fall."

I loved my sister, but I was eager for a friend whose idea of a good time was something besides making hollyhock skirts for clothespin dolls.

Mrs. Larter said, "Of course it's just a one-room schoolhouse."

"A one-room schoolhouse?" Aunt Maude's eyebrows flew up. "Surely the girls could be taken to the school in the nearby town."

"Oh, dear, no," the women all said nearly at once.

Mrs. Thurston explained, "You can't imagine what the winters are like up here. The snow falls until there is nothing left to see but the tops of the trees. If the girls tried to travel into town, they might get to school in the morning and not be able to return home for a week.

They'll have to attend the country school."

With the excitement of snowstorms to come and the novelty of attending a whole schoolhouse contained all in one room, I couldn't wait for winter. But until that time there was still summer to get through, and summer meant Aunt Maude.

Carlie and I considered Aunt Maude as menacing as a hornets' nest, and we learned to keep our distance. While Carlie turned to Eleanor, I opened a book. But Aunt Maude was a terrible trouble to Eleanor. She had a great need to tell people how they must improve, and since Carlie and I were stubborn and would not listen, she concentrated on trying to improve Eleanor. Papa frowned upon these criticisms. "She is doing her best, Maude," Papa said, so Aunt Maude did not criticize Eleanor when Papa was near.

Aunt Maude refused to see how hard Eleanor tried— how she polished the dining room table until it shone; how she made gingerbread, knowing it was a favorite of Carlie's; how she struggled to make the dainty cucumber sandwiches Aunt Maude liked with her afternoon tea. Nothing Eleanor did satisfied Aunt Maude. Eleanor did not air the beds before making them, or the airing took too long and the beds were not made in a timely fashion. The piecrust was too tough or too crumbly.

Eleanor forgot to put down crumpled damp newspaper to catch the dust before she swept, or she wasted too much newspaper in the crumpling.

It seemed the harder Eleanor tried to please Aunt Maude, the more fault Aunt Maude found with her. Once, after one of Aunt Maude's scoldings, I came upon Eleanor crying. When I asked what the matter was, she quickly began peeling an onion and blamed it for the tears.

Eleanor often looked longingly out the window. When I asked what she was looking at, she said, "The out-of-doors. I feel like I am stuck inside someone's pocket. At the farm on a day like this," she said with a sigh, "I'd be picking the first strawberries. We always picked before breakfast, when the berries were still plump with the dew and the sun hadn't turned hot." Instead Eleanor had to stay in the kitchen, kneading a great lump of dough, for Aunt Maude had taken a dislike to the bread put out by the asylum bakery and wanted Eleanor to bake bread according to Aunt Maude's own recipe. The woodstove was fired up, and waves of heat settled in the kitchen.

Carlie and I were free to escape into the July day.

"Why does Aunt Maude scold Eleanor all the time?" Carlie asked.

"I don't know," I said, but that wasn't exactly true.

Aunt Maude was stingy with her love and thought other people were too. She seemed to believe that if Carlie and I loved Eleanor, we wouldn't have enough love left over for her. I noticed that when Carlie shadowed Eleanor around the house, Aunt Maude would find a way to get Carlie's attention and draw her away from Eleanor. That gave me an idea, the first good idea I'd had on how to get rid of Aunt Maude. I'd tell Carlie not to be shy about letting Aunt Maude see how much she preferred being with Eleanor to being with her. Perhaps Aunt Maude would be so jealous of Eleanor that she would leave.

THREE

In our eagerness to escape Aunt Maude, Carlie and I were out of the house after breakfast each day and on our way to the cow barn to see the cows milked. The barn was lit with lanterns that cast shadows of giant cows on the walls. It smelled of milk and hay and animals and was full of the cows' restless shuffling and warmth. Carlie loved to play with the cats and kittens that were kept in the barn to hunt mice.

We followed the wagons that carted the milk from the barn to the dairy. The dairy was cool on even the warmest day, for gallons of cold well water flowed through the contraption that separated the cream from the milk. The cream was then churned into hundreds of pounds of butter. From the dairy, wagons carried the milk and butter to the asylum kitchens.

While the dairy was cool, the asylum laundry was so hot that Carlie would not go into it. "It makes me melt," she complained. The patients who had to work there gathered outside the building on their breaks, their faces shining with sweat, their damp clothes clinging to their backs. They drank gallons of water, and I had seen them on a dare, giggling and full of mischief, tip the water pails over one another.

All the food for the patients was grown on the farm. The fields with their rows of corn and lettuce and tomatoes and carrots were like a market. There was a cannery, where vegetables were put up to feed the patients in the winter. There was a piggery, where we were allowed to hold the small piglets that struggled in our arms until they slipped out and went squealing to their mothers. There was a butchery, but we never went there. Whenever I thought of it, I had bad dreams.

The most amazing place was the series of heated glasshouses where flowers lived in rooms like people. Patients worked there. Our favorite gardener was Louis. He was grandfather old, with a stoop to his shoulders from leaning over the glasshouse benches and the flower beds. He had brown eyes that were magnified by his glasses and got even bigger when he was talking about his flowers. He was always on the lookout for bugs, and when he found them, he squeezed them to death between his bare fingers. Louis was always happy to answer my questions.

"Do you sell the flowers?" I asked.

"Oh, no, miss," he said. "When a garden looks a little bare, we tuck new plants in, but most of the flowers we send up to the asylum. Before I was myself again, it was what I looked forward to. I liked to guess what would turn up. I favored the snapdragons. When I was well enough to work, I said, 'Send me to the flowers.'"

Though Louis appeared very gentle, he told us that he had come to the asylum because he had sent letters to the governor and the congressmen in our state and to the president in Washington. "I told them what I thought of them, told them what I was going to do to them too if they didn't pay attention to what I said." He looked sheepish. "Guess I got a little carried away. I still write my letters, but they won't let me mail them." He looked around to see if anyone was watching. "I got one right here to President McKinley. Be a good girl, Verna, and mail it for me." Before I could refuse, he hastily tucked it into the pocket of my pinafore and scurried away.

"You're going to mail it for him, aren't you?" Carlie asked. Louis always sent Carlie home with a fistful of blooms. "There are stamps in Papa's study."

"I don't think I should mail it without showing it to Papa."

"If you do that, you'll get Louis into trouble."

I thought for a minute. "I'll show it to Eleanor. She'll know what to do."

Eleanor unfolded the letter and read it out to us:

Dear President McKinley,

I am a veteran of the Civil War and fought for my country, which is now in trouble because someone, and I ain't saying who, is sending birds to watch me. The birds are up in the trees looking in my window and watching me when I'm working. I'm not going to do anything to the birds because it ain't their fault, but look out in Washington, D.C.

Yours truly,
Louis Snartler

"I'll tell you what," Eleanor said, "Let's just pretend the woodstove is a mailbox. That way Louis isn't going to get into any trouble. We don't want any policemen from Washington coming here and looking for him."

"What will you tell Louis?" Carlie asked me.

"I'll think of something." It seemed to me that Louis

was making things up a little like the authors who wrote the books I loved to read.

A few days later, when we saw Louis again, he said, "Well, that letter I told you about got some action. There's a whole new set of birds up there, and they ain't paying me any attention." So everything turned out all right.

If Aunt Maude was making calls on the wives of the doctors, we sometimes stayed at home with Eleanor. Carlie and I would beg Eleanor to tell us what the asylum was like inside, for the great building was a mystery. Eleanor would not stop working but chatted on as she peeled potatoes or polished the silver. "It's cozy, really. They keep everything spotless, and there are even white tablecloths in the dining rooms, something I never saw at our farm. Flowers are set about on the tables, and there are pots of ivy hanging from the ceiling so you feel you are in a fairy forest. They have dances for the patients and card parties, and once they took us out and let us fly kites. That was my favorite day. I was still on the locked ward then, and it was such a treat to see those kites up in the sky, free as could be, but still they had that string to fall back on so they wouldn't just drift away."

Eleanor lowered her voice as though someone might overhear her. "Of course, the back wards are not so nice. The patients there are what they call disturbed, and they break things. You couldn't have vases of flowers about on the back wards. I was there just for a few days when I first came. That's where I met Lucy Anster, who was my special friend. We were both in a bad way. I was crying all the time, and Lucy kept finding a way to hurt herself. Lucy is still there, but they soon had me to rights, and here I am. The doctor says if I keep improving, I might get to visit the farm and see my brother, Tom, and my mom and dad. I'm lonesome for my mother and Tom."

"Not your dad?" I asked.

"He's like your aunt Maude. Nothing I do pleases him." Eleanor quickly looked around. "I shouldn't say anything against your aunt. I'm sure she means well, and she's taught me how to take care of all your nice things." Eleanor gave the silver teapot an extra buffing.

"I think she's mean to you," Carlie said. "She's always scolding you."

Eleanor's shoulders drooped, and tears formed in the corners of her eyes. "I'm used to that. I got plenty of it from my dad. What's hard is being inside a house all day. Farm women like me are used to the screen door slamming. There's weeding and hoeing in the kitchen garden. Then there's the berry picking: raspberries on the farm and wild blueberries and blackberries off somewhere in the woods. Even in the winter there's breaking a trail through the snow to feed the chickens and collect eggs. Sometimes this house is like a collar that's too tight around my throat. I feel *eingeschlossen*."

Eleanor said that was German for "shut in" and got me a penny from Papa. I knew when I went to Papa, he would ask me where I had heard the word, and I was all prepared. I said, "That's how Eleanor feels because she misses being outside. Aunt Maude keeps her so busy, she can't even sit on the porch steps for a breath of fresh air."

That evening I was delighted to hear Papa instruct Aunt Maude, "You must give Eleanor an hour off every afternoon."

Aunt Maude bristled. "I never heard of such a thing, letting the help have a holiday like that."

Papa was firm. "One hour a day is not too large a price to pay if it helps Eleanor to recover from her illness."

"This house is not part of the asylum," Aunt Maude insisted.

Papa had the last word. "That is just what it is."

From then on, when the dinner dishes were done, the vegetables were scrubbed for supper, and the table was set, Eleanor burst out of the house with Carlie holding one hand and me the other. Aunt Maude stood wistfully at the kitchen window, watching as we ran off.

There was always something new to see when we were with Eleanor. She discovered things where anyone else might just pass right by without a second look: a cocoon attached to a branch, or the shape of the holes a woodpecker made in a tree, or a little patch of violets hidden in the grass. Eleanor's favorite place was the small lake at the edge of the asylum fields. We could walk all around it in half an hour. It was called Mud Lake, but Carlie said that was an ugly name. She called it Green Lake, for in the afternoons the reflection of the trees that ringed the shore made the water a deep green.

We had not been allowed to go there unless someone was with us. Aunt Maude would not go, and Papa was too busy, so we were exploring the lake for the first time. There was a beaver lodge on the lake, and Eleanor said if we got down on our hands and knees, we could smell the musky odor of the animals inside, and that was true. The beavers, who slept all day, woke up when they heard us. They swam out into the lake and hit the water with their tails to make an explosion. Eleanor said, "It's their way of warning the other beavers that strangers are nearby."

When it was hot, we took off our shoes and socks and, holding up our skirts, waded in the water, feeling the soft mud ooze up between our toes. Eleanor made us stay close to shore. She warned, "If you give it a chance, that mud sucks at you like hands grabbing hold of you and pulling you down."

Sometimes we would scare up a heron. The heron was nearly as tall as Carlie, and after she saw it spear a frog with its cruel beak, Carlie hated the bird. Eleanor showed us raccoon tracks and the empty clamshells the raccoons had left behind after their midnight supper. Carlie, who could not see a thing without picking it up and taking it home, collected the shells for doll dishes. I gathered snail shells, and Eleanor showed me how to make a hole in each and string them for bracelets. Like the wild berries we picked, the shells were just there, gifts, and you didn't even have to be good to get them—which was just as well, because I knew I was not being good. I was going out of my way to make Aunt Maude see how much more Carlie and I liked being with Eleanor than we liked being with her. I hoped she would take the hint and go back home.

Each afternoon Eleanor's hour flew by, but no amount of coaxing kept her too long at the lake, for once we had been a couple of minutes late in getting back and found Aunt Maude standing on the pack porch, a hand shading her eyes, watching for us. "If you are late again, Eleanor," she said, "you will take your rest hour here in the house."

FOUR

We had been at the asylum two weeks when an invitation came for us to have supper on a Friday evening with Dr. Thurston and his wife. Carlie was to stay home with Eleanor to watch her, but I was invited. Carlie didn't care. "I'd rather stay with Eleanor," she declared. Ordinarily I would have felt the same way. I didn't look forward to an hour of having to sit up straight, eat everything on my plate, and make polite conversation, but the Thurstons lived in the asylum, so at last I would have a glimpse inside the mysterious building.

Aunt Maude was torn between the honor of being invited for supper by the asylum's superintendent and her conviction that it would be dangerous to set foot inside the building. "How can the Thurstons bear to spend their days among such people?" Aunt Maude asked.

Papa gave Aunt Maude a twisty smile. "You forget, Maude, that is exactly what I do, and I don't believe I am any the worse for it."

"But to live in that building, day and night. What can it be like?"

"I think you will be surprised at the Thurstons' home, Maude," Papa said.

Aunt Maude dragged her heels on the way to the asylum and had to be coaxed to go through the massive entrance. Once we got inside, Papa indicated two locked doors on either side of the entrance hall. "Those are the wards," he said.

I thought of Eleanor and her word *eingeschlossen*, shut in. However pleasant it might be inside the wards, however many white tablecloths and flowers and baskets of ivy, still Eleanor must hear the key in the lock.

Papa led us up a sweeping stairway. We were greeted by Dr. and Mrs. Thurston and a small black Scotch terrier that turned excited circles in welcome. Dr. Thurston had white hair, a pointed white beard that wagged as he talked, and bright blue eyes that looked hard at you. Mrs. Thurston, like Aunt Maude, was a large woman, but where Aunt Maude's figure was trussed up by stiff corsets,

Mrs. Thurston overflowed into soft bundles in front and behind. Her hair was piled into a great puff, and a long necklace of jet beads like shiny black beetles stretched down the front of her green silk dress. She extended one welcoming hand to Aunt Maude and another to me.

"How I have looked forward to having Edward and his sister-in-law and his dear daughter as our guests, Miss Wingate. You will see that since I call Edward by his first name, we are already on friendly terms. Dr. Thurston has only good things to say about Edward's work with the patients. Now let me show you our little nest."

The little nest was pleasant and spacious, with a large parlor, a library, and a study for Dr. Thurston. Down the halls we could see several bedrooms. The parlor where we settled was handsomely furnished with fine pictures on the walls and pretty ornaments set out on the tables. Aunt Maude was clearly impressed. Still, she asked in a kind of whisper, as if she could be overheard in the nearby wards, "But what of the patients? Aren't you worried about having them so close by?"

"Heavens, no," Mrs. Thurston said. "It is very convenient for Dr. Thurston, and as for me, I have become quite friendly with many of the poor souls."

I was sure Mrs. Thurston meant well, but I was glad Eleanor was not there to hear her. I certainly did not think of Eleanor as a poor soul but as a good friend.

At supper I had to sit quietly with nothing to do but bury my peas in my mashed potatoes and discover them again while I listened to Dr. Thurston set forth his theories. He said, "I am sure there is a relationship between a patient's surroundings and the patient's mental state. If beauty is around us, beauty will be in us. I spared no expense in the building of this asylum. The hallways are spacious. The windows are barred, yes, but they are wide and high, flooding the rooms with light. The patients look out at green fields, flowers, winding paths, newly planted trees and shrubbery. There is even a garden with a fountain, available to the more disturbed patients. The garden is locked, of course, but that is for the patients' protection."

So that was what the locked garden was for. I thought it was nice that there was a garden for the very sick patients, but no matter how lovely it was, the iron bars of the fence must remind them of the bars on their windows.

"People come from all over to see our asylum and tramp about the paths," Dr. Thurston was going on. "We have had classrooms of students arrive with their picnic baskets to enjoy the grounds."

I knew that was true, because only the other day I had

seen a family gathered in the shade of some maple trees, the mother handing around cookies and glasses of lemonade to several small children. I thought it must make the patients feel better to see that visitors liked coming there and weren't afraid of the asylum, but then the visitors could go back home and the patients had to stay.

Beneath the table the Scotch terrier was nibbling at my shoelaces. I took up a bit of buttered roll, and letting my hand drop first to my lap and then under the tablecloth, I gave the piece of roll to the terrier.

Dr. Thurston was boasting, "On the wards there are pictures on the walls and fresh flowers daily. Many of our patients come to us from miserable conditions, from unhappy homes with no refinements, from poor farms and city slums. We open up a new world of grace and beauty. Our state has provided a hospital for our patients that is an asylum in every sense of the word."

I knew Papa would not be content just to listen, for I had heard him declare there was more to be done than to lock people away, no matter how nice the wards were. Sure enough, Papa interrupted Dr. Thurston to say, "I grant you that melancholy patients or those who have been abused at home will improve if removed from their troubled surroundings and will respond to the pleasant setting of the asylum. But what of those in the back wards who don't notice such things? You must admit that because you refuse to allow straitjackets, such patients are managed only by strong doses of morphine. That is not a cure. What use are the pretty pictures and trees and flowers to such patients?"

I saw that Dr. Thurston did not like to be reminded of such things, but he was very fair to Papa and said only, "Of course there are exceptions, patients who cannot be reached by beauty alone, but I am convinced that even in their disturbed state it has some effect. It is like the chameleon who takes on the color of its surroundings. It does not do so consciously, but it survives in the doing."

Papa was not to be quieted and boldly said, "But why should there not be medicine for the mind as there is for the body?"

Mrs. Thurston must have seen that there was to be no stopping the two men, for she stood up, saying, "Maude and Verna and I will leave the two of you to argue while we have our after-supper coffee." With the Scotch terrier, whose name I learned was Macduff, trailing after me in the hope of more buttered roll, we returned to the parlor, where the maid who had served us supper brought us a silver tray with tiny cups of coffee for Mrs. Thurston and Aunt Maude and cocoa for me. On the tray were little cakes with the sugared violets Aunt Maude despised.

Aunt Maude said, "Your maid is so efficient and so stately. I envy you. We have only a farm girl, and a patient at that."

"But our maid is a patient as well," Mrs. Thurston said.

"But what is wrong with Eleanor?" Aunt Maude asked. "Why did she come to the asylum?"

I had been scratching Macduff's ears, but now I stopped to listen, for I wondered the same thing.

Mrs. Thurston was about to answer, but she paused and for a moment looked intently at Aunt Maude. What she saw there must have changed her mind, for she only said, "Whatever it was, I am sure Eleanor is doing very well, and you are lucky to have her. Now, here come the gentlemen to join us. Let us see if we can get Dr. Thurston to forget his theories long enough to allow us a little music. You would not know to look at him that he has a fine tenor voice." She smiled fondly at him and, seating herself at the piano, asked Aunt Maude if she would join Dr. Thurston in a song or two.

"Heavens, no. I have no talent along those lines, but my brother-in-law has an excellent voice. My dear dead sister, Isabel, would play and Edward would sing. I'm afraid, Edward, that you have not been able to bring yourself to sing again."

Papa said, "I am sure Isabel would not have wished that I give up singing." He stood by the piano and in his fine deep voice joined Dr. Thurston in some German songs that I did not understand but that made Aunt Maude and Mrs. Thurston wipe tears from their eyes and sent Macduff under a chair.

Mrs. Thurston turned to me and said, "Verna, I understand from your father that you play the piano. Would you play something for us?"

I didn't know what to do. While Aunt Maude said a lady should never put herself forward, Papa said it was false modesty to have to be coaxed. I took a deep breath and advanced toward the piano. Aunt Maude frowned, and Papa gave me an encouraging smile. I played Beethoven's "Für Elise" and got through it with just two mistakes. Everyone applauded, even Aunt Maude.

As we were leaving, Mrs. Thurston said, "Edward, there is a chapel in the asylum with services for the patients each Sunday. Dr. Thurston and I make it a point to attend. I play the organ. I hope you will sing in the choir."

Papa said, "I would be happy to."

Mrs. Thurston looked pleased. "You will find that

many of the patients have fine voices, none of them finer than your very own Eleanor."

At that Aunt Maude looked stormy. I could not tell whether it was because Mrs. Thurston had called her "your very own Eleanor" or because Papa was going to sing in the same choir as the patients.

FIVE

R eturning home from our supper with the Thurstons, I ran on ahead. Sitting so long with grown-ups had made me fidgety. When I got to our house, Eleanor was at the door waiting, a frightened look on her face. She scarcely said hello to me but kept her eye on Aunt Maude.

"Is Carlie asleep?" I asked.

Eleanor nodded and looked more unhappy than ever.

Papa was just sending me off to bed when we heard Aunt Maude's angry voice. I followed Papa into the dining room, where Aunt Maude was scolding Eleanor. Aunt Maude turned to us. "It's Isabel's glass punch bowl. There is a chip in it. I have told Eleanor never to touch it, and now just see what has happened."

Eleanor had made herself very small. Her face was as red as her hands, and there were tears running down her cheeks. "I'm so sorry, ma'am. It's my fault."

"You don't belong in a decent home. You don't know how to handle nice things."

Papa put a hand on Aunt Maude's shoulder. "Let us give Eleanor credit for pointing the accident out to you. Now I think we should hear what Eleanor has to say." He waited for Eleanor to tell her story, but Eleanor only shook her head, repeating that it was her fault.

I noticed a puddle of water snaking out from under the dining room table. Papa saw it too. He pulled up the tablecloth to find Carlie's stuffed rabbit, Promise. It was soaking wet.

Papa said, "Verna, go upstairs and get your sister out of bed."

Carlie wasn't in bed. She was standing at the top of the stairway, her lower lip caught between her teeth and her forehead all scrunched up. It was how she would look just before she began to cry. She followed me down the stairway but had to be coaxed, sobbing, into the dining room.

Papa put an arm around her. "Caroline, tell me the truth. Did you take the punch bowl down from the sideboard?"

Carlie nodded her head yes.

"And then what happened?" Papa asked.

Between sobs, Carlie said, "I was in bed, but Promise was getting the bed dirty because he was all sandy, so I came downstairs and got the big bowl to give Promise a bath in. When I went to put it back, it was slippery. It jumped out of my hands."

Aunt Maude turned to Eleanor. "Where were you when this happened?"

"I thought Carlie was asleep in her bed. It was such a nice night that I sat on the back steps and watched for falling stars. I never should have gone outside. It's all my fault."

"You are not to be trusted with children," Aunt Maude said.

Papa looked angry. "Of course Eleanor is to be trusted. Caroline had no business getting out of bed. Now, girls, I want you upstairs at once. Eleanor, you go along home to the asylum, and remember, this was not your fault."

After Eleanor left, Aunt Maude said, "That was Isabel's favorite bowl. I don't know how you can make light of it."

Papa said, "Maude, a chipped bowl is not the end of the world. I am sure Isabel would agree with me."

As Carlie and I went up the stairs, I heard an angry Aunt Maude say, "You took that woman's part against me."

Papa replied, "There is no taking of parts. There is only speaking the truth. This is not the first time I have had to explain to you, Maude, that Eleanor is very sensitive to criticism. There has been too much of it in her past."

After what had happened, I was afraid that Eleanor would not return, but the next morning when I awoke, I smelled pancakes. Aunt Maude seldom made pancakes. Eleanor was careful in all she did that morning, handling the dishes as if they were eggshells and saying little. Aunt Maude was on her best behavior as well. I heard her say to Eleanor, in a voice that sounded like it had been pushed through a sieve, "Perhaps I was a little hasty last night in what I said to you."

Quickly Eleanor replied, "I'm truly sorry about the bowl. If it can be repaired, you could take the cost out of my salary."

Aunt Maude said, "There will be no need for that." But Aunt Maude, being Aunt Maude, could not keep from adding, "I only wish it had not been that *special* bowl."

The next day was a Sunday, and Eleanor didn't come on Sundays. Aunt Maude made us fried eggs for breakfast. The centers were hard, and Carlie whispered to me, "Aunt Maude killed the eggs again." After we had eaten, Carlie and I put on our hats and white gloves and followed Aunt Maude to the asylum chapel. Papa had left early to take his place in the choir.

Both Carlie and I looked forward to church, because we always heard a new word or two from the pulpit that meant pennies. The asylum chapel was a small copy of the church that we used to attend. The patients were neatly dressed in what looked to be their best clothes. With the exception of a few who slunk down in their pews or looked suspiciously about, the churchgoers appeared perfectly normal. A minister stood at the pulpit, talking away. While we listened for words, Carlie poked her fingers into and out of her gloves, and I tried to twist my straight hair into curls. The choir, all wearing identical white robes, was seated to one side of the altar. I spotted Papa and Eleanor at once and, catching Papa's eye, winked at him, causing Aunt Maude to nudge me.

Eleanor sang a solo, "Jerusalem." It was a hymn I loved. Imagining its "chariot of fire" appearing through the clouds sent shivers down my spine. Mrs. Thurston was right. Eleanor's voice was like a glass of cool water on a hot day. I happened to look at Papa while Eleanor was singing and saw that he was staring at Eleanor. On his face was the look he got when there was an article in one of his journals that interested him. Aunt Maude noticed the look too. Her mouth formed a tight line, and her hands clenched until the knuckles whitened.

On the way home I collected a penny for *aspire*. Carlie got a penny for *damnation*, which I think she chose because she could say the *damn* part.

"Really, Edward," Aunt Maude said, "I cannot understand your paying those children for words."

Papa said, "Teaching children that there is a value in words, Maude, cannot be a bad thing."

Even though it was July and ninety degrees out, Aunt Maude always gave us the same Sunday dinner: roast pork, applesauce, mashed potatoes, carrots, and peas. Carlie was separating her carrots from her peas, I was mixing the applesauce with the gravy, and Aunt Maude had just opened her mouth to tell us to stop playing with our food when Papa said, "Maude, on such a warm day you needn't take trouble over a hot dinner. A little salad and a sandwich are all we need."

Aunt Maude got red right down to her neck. She always treated Papa's suggestions as if he were criticizing her. "I'm sorry you don't care for your dinner, Edward. I notice you don't seem to have any problem with your appetite when it's Eleanor cooking."

Papa looked startled. He hadn't seen Aunt Maude watch him while Eleanor was singing. "Whatever can you mean, Maude? You know that I enjoy your meals. I am only remarking on the suitability of a large hot meal in this warm weather." After that it was so quiet, you could hear everyone chew and swallow.

Before we could escape the hot kitchen, I had to dry the dishes and Carlie had to put the silverware away. Since Carlie had to have all the spoons and forks fit one another just so, that took a long time. When we were finally outside, Carlie and I wandered over the asylum grounds. We stopped to watch a bee lose itself inside an orange lily. A hummingbird mistook Carlie's flowered sunbonnet for a blossom. Where a geranium or pansy had wilted, a gardener was substituting a fresh plant. Most of the gardeners were patients, and their faces were familiar to us. They interrupted their work to call out a pleasant greeting.

Louis was working outside on this afternoon instead of in the glasshouses. He was bent into a grasshopper shape, clipping grass around a flower bed, and took his time straightening up. Putting a finger over his mouth, he quietly tiptoed to a maple tree, signaling us to follow. A little way up the tree was a robin's nest cleverly fashioned of bits of birch bark and grass stuck together with mud. Four open beaks poked up from the nest. "I find plenty of worms in my digging," Louis said, "but I wouldn't chew the worms up even for them little fellows." He winked at me. "I got the birds all on my side now," he said.

The last time we had seen Louis, he had promised to bring his medal from the Civil War to show us. Now he took it out of his pocket. It was wrapped up in a square of cotton. "I was with the Army of the Cumberland," he said, "following General Rosecrans back and forth across the Tennessee River. After I was shot, I was in a hospital. You couldn't sleep what with the moans all around you. The floor was slippery with blood, and there was legs that had been cut off all piled up. I still have nightmares."

I didn't want to hear any more, but Carlie asked, "What happened to all the cut-off legs?"

Louis grinned at her. "They just walked off." He noticed the expression on my face. "It wasn't all so bad. We was bivouacked not far from the Tennessee River. By the camp the river was littered with garbage and filth. But a mile upstream the water was pure. Willow trees hung over the river; whippoorwills called. Miserable as the fighting was, once I could get away for a bit to the river, I was fine. That's how it is here at the asylum. I hate it inside, but once I get outside and get my hands in some dirt, I'm fine."

He bent down and began snipping again. "I got to tend to the grass. The flowers don't mean as much to

Dr. Thurston as his grass. It's as if this little green piece of the world is one thing he can have just the way he wants. All day long he has to do with us patients in the asylum and our difficult ways; then he comes out here and sees the perfect green lawn. He'll stand here and look at it as if he was a drowning man and it was a boat."

Carlie complained of the heat, and we left the path for the acres of trees that made little pools of shade. A figure came from behind a tree. "Well, it must be Caroline, and here is Verna as well." It was Dr. Thurston himself. He seemed pleased to find us exploring the grounds. "Have you ever seen such a beautiful lawn? And what do you make of my little forest?"

"I know the maples and the birches and the pines," I said, "but there are trees I've never seen before."

"Whenever I take a trip, I send a tree back. Two years ago Mrs. Thurston and I traveled to Japan and China. This mulberry tree is grown in Japan, where its bark is used to make paper, and that mulberry tree over there is grown in China and its leaves are fed to the silkworms. Look here." He led us to a strange willow tree whose branches were twisted into corkscrew shapes. "This tree grew from a twig I brought all the way from Nanking, keeping it watered while we traveled thousands of miles by cart and ship."

"But how did you get it up through the hole?" Carlie asked. Someone had once told her that China was at the bottom of the world and you had to dig right through the earth to the other side to get there.

Dr. Thurston smiled. "Well, it wasn't easy." He gave the willow a friendly pat. "I have never seen such natural beauty as I saw in China. Willows are planted along the rivers so that their tresses lean over the water like women washing their hair." His face reddened. "You have caught me in a poetic mood, children. I must beg you not to tell on me. Your father will think I am too much a romantic to be a scientist, but it gave me great pleasure to think of bringing back to my patients some of the beauty I had experienced."

We came upon the little garden with the iron fence and the fountain.

Carlie, who had not heard Dr. Thurston's explanation at the supper table, asked, "Why is the garden locked?"

"Sadly, my dear, there are patients who are not well enough to roam freely. Yet it is important that they have the advantage of nature's beauty. Nature, Carlie, is the mother that heals. Your father, fine scientist that he is, may look for a medicine to cure the terrible ills of the mind, but I say that we must surround our patients with beauty, and nature will do the rest."

Carlie was not to be put off by fine talk. "Is the hole you made to get to China still there?"

"Ah, no. I'm afraid we had to fill it up so that no one would accidentally fall in."

After he left us, I thought over Dr. Thurston's ideas. It was all very well for the gardeners who worked outside and for the patients who strolled along the paths of the asylum, but what of patients in the back wards and even those like Eleanor who were confined to long hours cooking and cleaning and didn't have much chance to be cured by nature?

I knew how much Eleanor missed being outside. She often spoke longingly of her family's farm. The doctors had finally given her permission to make a visit to her parents, who lived close by, but Aunt Maude could not find a time when Eleanor was not badly needed, which was strange to me, for when speaking of Eleanor, Aunt Maude referred to her as "useless." I did not see how she could be both necessary and useless.

At the end of July Eleanor finally got to see her family, for Aunt Maude received a letter calling her away. The family that rented her house while she stayed with us was moving. She needed to return home for a week or two to see about preparing the house for new renters.

"I don't see how I can leave you," she told Papa.

"Eleanor will be no good at all without my supervision. You must not let her get into sloppy ways."

Papa assured her that we could manage. I said nothing at all, for I knew my pleasure at her leaving would show and Papa would not like that. Carlie said, "What if you get lost, Auntie Maude, and can't find your way back?" Aunt Maude could not mistake the hope in Carlie's voice. Carlie's happy expression as she watched Aunt Maude pack and my eager offers of assistance must have told Aunt Maude that Carlie and I were looking forward to her leaving.

Aunt Maude looked up from her packing and startled us by saying, "I'm afraid, girls, that I have not earned your affections."

I was embarrassed to see two tears start down her cheeks. I hurried to say, "Aunt Maude, I am sure we appreciate all you have done for us."

"It's not appreciation I want, Verna."

Aunt Maude was asking for our love. Sometimes you are asked for something you might be able to give, but you will not give it. I have had two cookies in my hand while Carlie has gobbled down hers. When she pleaded for one of mine, I could have given it to her, but I told myself she didn't deserve it. I said to myself now that Aunt Maude had not deserved my love, and when she asked for it, I was silent.

Carlie, who was so greedy and must have everything she saw, stored it all up and gave it back without a thought. Now she thrust her stuffed rabbit at Aunt Maude, the rabbit that Carlie would not let out of her sight. "You can take Promise to keep you company," she said.

Aunt Maude smiled, the first real smile I remembered seeing on her face. "Thank you, Carlie. I won't need the rabbit, for I will have the memory of your kindness."

Eleanor made herself very small and quiet, and we held our breaths until the day the carriage drove up and Aunt Maude, after many cautions to Eleanor and to me and Carlie, and after many false starts, reluctantly climbed in and was carried away.

SIX

Without Aunt Maude the house felt light, as if it might float away. Eleanor sang as she worked. Papa dared to smoke his pipe in the front parlor. I wore my hair loose around my shoulders instead of in the tight braids Aunt Maude insisted on, which pinched and made my head ache. Carlie stopped wearing shoes altogether. Eleanor baked our favorite chocolate cake with fudge frosting so thick, I could stick my finger into it all the way up to my second knuckle. Since there were only three of us at the dining room table, Papa told Eleanor to join us. She hesitated, but the second time Papa asked, she slipped shyly onto a chair.

One evening after the supper dishes were done, I asked Eleanor if she would stay and sing while I played piano. At first she shook her head and only stood there, listening to me. The music must have been too much for her, for she kept time with her toe, and when I coaxed, she began to sing, quietly at first and then with all her heart. Carlie danced. Papa left his study and after a moment joined in the singing. For the first time since Mama had died, it felt like we were a family again.

After that Eleanor stayed each evening and Papa stopped spending so much of his time on *The Closed Door*. At first we all sang Stephen Foster melodies and other familiar tunes, but Papa, who loved lieder, which was what he called German songs, taught Eleanor his favorites. Since she knew German to begin with, she caught on quickly. When it was time for Eleanor to go home, Carlie and I walked back to the asylum with her, singing all the way there and back. With Aunt Maude gone, our whole life had turned into music.

Aunt Maude wrote every day, so we were always opening a letter from her to find a long list of what must be dusted and cooked and turned out and scrubbed. Papa and I dutifully read the letters and then folded them up and put them back into their envelopes, the way you might put your hand over the mouth of someone whose words you did not want to hear.

Aunt Maude had been gone a week when Papa gave

Eleanor permission to take a day off to visit her parents. The Miller farm was an hour's buggy drive away. Her brother would pick her up in the morning and return with her after supper. I had heard so many stories from Eleanor of the farm, I longed to see it. When Eleanor suggested that Carlie and I accompany her, I begged Papa to let us go. I knew that after Aunt Maude returned, there would be no going off with Eleanor. Papa, who was never one to hurry into a decision, took a whole day to think about it and then said we might go if we promised to do just as Eleanor said and not be a trouble to anyone.

The following morning Eleanor and I were sitting on the porch a whole hour before her brother, Tom, was expected. We were listening to the cicadas. For days the air had quivered with the insects' whining song, but when I looked for them, I could never find them. They were all song and no body. Carlie was nearby, chasing a rabbit that had been nibbling on the clover that grew in thick patches on the lawn. Papa had told Carlie that if she caught the rabbit, she might keep it, but the rabbit would not be caught.

It was the first day of August. The daisies had disappeared, and goldenrod grew along the roadside. The leaves on Dr. Thurston's trees had a dusty look, and in the asylum fields the potatoes had begun to blossom, and the corn to tassel.

Just when I thought it would never appear, the Millers' buggy with two shaggy, tired-looking horses pulled up, driven by Eleanor's brother. Tom was eighteen, slim like Eleanor, but tall, and brown as any hardworking farmer would be. He gave Carlie and me and our house and everything else a close, serious look, as if he were a little wary of it all. I could see he wanted to give Eleanor a hug but was shy in front of me. Eleanor ignored his shyness and threw her arms around him. Though they weren't her brothers, she threw her arms around the horses as well and fed them sugar cubes.

Papa, who had stayed at home to see us off, came out of the house and shook hands with Tom. "Don't let the horses run away with you," Papa said. His face was perfectly serious, but I could see he was teasing.

Tom, not sure of how to take Papa, said, "Those horses are steady, sir."

"Horses are only as steady as the man with the reins," Papa said.

I laughed. "Papa, don't be a goose. I'm sure Tom will take good care of us."

When we were a distance from our house, Tom said, "If I called our dad a goose, he'd knock me down."

"You mean he would hit you?" I asked, amazed.

"Sure, he would, and it wouldn't be the first time."

The four of us were crowded together on the wagon seat, Carlie on Eleanor's lap. Eleanor asked, "Tom, is Dad still angry with me?"

"Yes, but he doesn't talk about it much anymore."

Eleanor breathed a sigh of relief. "That's something."

"Why should he be angry with you?" Carlie asked.

"He can't forgive me for being sick." She hastily changed the subject and began to point out to Tom the fields of corn that stretched as far as we could see. "That all belongs to the asylum, Tom. They have three silos. They get hundreds of bushels of corn, and they have an orchard with cherry trees and apple and pear and plum trees."

Tom, who had seemed nervous at first as we drove by the asylum, now took an interest. "How many cows have they got?" he asked.

I knew the answer to that from my visits to the barns. "Four hundred head of Holsteins," I said.

Tom whistled. "I wouldn't mind being a little crazy myself if I could work here."

Carlie said, "Papa says we shouldn't say the word *crazy*."

"Sorry," he said, and put his arm around Eleanor for

a moment. "I'm glad you're coming home, Elly, even if it's just for a day."

When we reached the farm, Eleanor hopped out of the buggy before it came to a stop. Her mother was standing at the back door, watching for us, her hand above her eyes to shield them from the sun. In a minute she had her arms around Eleanor and hung on to her for dear life. At last Carlie and I were introduced, and we shook hands with Mrs. Miller.

She looked closely at us, as if she had never seen children before, which was strange because she had two of her own. "I'm sure you are very welcome," she said. She had a German accent, and I remembered that Eleanor had said her mother had come to this country as a girl from Germany. "Your daddy is a doctor, I know, and your poor mama died," she went on. I guessed that Eleanor had written home about us.

"Where is Dad?" Eleanor asked.

"He's out in the potato field. We've got some kind of blight this year. I don't know if we'll harvest half the crop. After we put what we need aside, I doubt there will be much left over to sell."

Eleanor seemed relieved that her father wasn't there. She dragged Carlie and me along to see the cows, rubbing her face against the muzzle of a new calf. The next minute she was off to the pigpen, where she had a name and a story for every pig. Her mother had to call her twice before she would go in to dinner. As we followed her about, we saw that she was a different person on the farm. Carlie whispered, "It's like the story where the prince kisses Snow White and she comes alive."

Dinner was at the kitchen table. Mr. Miller had come in from the potato field. He was a square and sturdy man, with Eleanor's silver blond hair, but not Eleanor's big eyes. His were small and darted about all the time as if some biting insect were trying to get at him. He pumped water into the sink and, taking up a little piece of brown soap, scrubbed at his hands as if he were angry with them. When Mrs. Miller introduced us, he only nodded his head, not even bothering to look up. While he dried his hands on the roller towel, he glanced over his shoulder at Eleanor.

"You look about the same," he said. "How come they let you out?"

Mrs. Miller quickly said, "You know the doctor told us Eleanor was better."

"Those aren't real doctors there," Mr. Miller said.

Carlie spoke up. "My papa is a real doctor."

"Does your father let you contradict your betters?" Mr. Miller's cold look silenced Carlie.

When we sat around the table with Papa, he always questioned us about what we had been doing, and we gave answers. The Millers mostly ate. Eleanor and her mother were up and down, serving the food: roast pork, mashed potatoes, peas, pickles, and for dessert, rhubarb pie and vinegar pie.

Tom glanced at his dad, who looked grouchy. "We'll be lucky if we get thirty-eight cents a bushel for oats this year," Tom said. His dad only shrugged.

When Mr. Miller finally did talk, he said something that upset Eleanor. "You better let me have your wages for the month—not that they give you a decent wage. I got a veterinary bill for one of the heifers and nothing to pay it with."

Eleanor blinked her eyes a couple of times to keep back tears. "I was saving to pay for a coat for the winter." There wasn't an ounce of hope in her voice.

"The vet won't come back unless I pay his bill. You want I should let the horses and cows die so you can buy a coat they'll probably never let you out long enough to wear?"

"Papa, I go out to Verna and Carlie's house every day to work."

"If you can work there, why can't you come home and give your mother a hand here?"

Eleanor said in a voice I could barely hear, "The doctor thinks I should stay a little longer."

"Sure he does. The asylum gets help for almost nothing. Why wouldn't they make you stay?"

Mrs. Miller cleared her throat as if she were going to say something, but in the end she didn't, and Eleanor said she'd send the money the next day. After the dishes were done, the table was wiped, and the dish towels were rinsed, Mrs. Miller said, "You wrote how nicely Verna plays piano, Elly. Let's have some music."

We all went into the parlor, where the Millers had an ancient upright piano. I played "Old Folks at Home," and Eleanor sang. Tom asked for "Camptown Races," and Mrs. Miller for "Beautiful Isle of Somewhere," whose sadness she enjoyed so much that it made her cry.

Mr. Miller sat through the performance restless as a chipmunk, crossing and recrossing his legs and cleaning out his pipe. He looked as though sitting still were a punishment. At last, with a thankful sigh, he said, "That'll do. Tom and me have to clean out the cream separator."

Eleanor led Carlie and me to the back of the farm, where woods sloped gently down a hill to the trickle of a creek. The creek was so narrow that Carlie could jump over it. Water striders skated over the top of the water.

"What are the orange flowers?" I asked.

"Touch-me-not," Eleanor said. "In the fall, if you touch the seedpods, the seeds explode into the air." She had brought an old chipped bowl with her, and now she began digging up some of the moss that grew along the edges of the creek. "I'm going to take it back with me. Feel how soft it is, Carlie." Carlie petted the green softness as if it were a kitten.

We sat on the bank of the stream in the afternoon sunshine. A robin darted down for a drink, stayed for a quick bath, and disappeared. "Do you mind giving your money to your dad?" I asked.

"What difference does it make if I mind?"

"What if you just didn't give it to him?" Carlie asked.

Eleanor shook her head. I could see that such a thing had never occurred to her. "I'm lucky he lets me come home at all."

I tried to think what it would be like to have Papa standing by the door, refusing to let us in. I saw myself turning away and creeping off. I wasn't really frightened, for I knew Papa would never behave like that, but it wasn't hard to imagine Mr. Miller sending Eleanor away.

When we returned to the farmhouse, Mrs. Miller sent Eleanor off to pick some blackberries for our supper. Carlie ran after her, and I started to follow, but Mrs. Miller stopped me. "Stay and help me set the table, Verna," she said.

I wanted to go with Eleanor, but I thought it would be impolite not to do what I was asked. When we were alone in the kitchen, Mrs. Miller said in a soft voice, "I wanted to keep you here to find out how my Eleanor is. I mean how she *really* is. Is the asylum a bad place? Are they good to her?"

I told her at once how pleasant the asylum was, describing the gardens and the wards with their pots of hanging ivy and vases of flowers. "Eleanor is with us all day. My aunt Maude is a little strict, but Papa and I are so pleased to have her, and I think she is happy with us."

"It hurt me so to see Eleanor go," Mrs. Miller said. "She was always the cheerful one around here. Of course she was young. I don't know too many women who have lived on a farm for fifty years and still find a lot to laugh about. When I was young like Eleanor, I took pleasure in the new leaves on the trees, the apple blossoms, the crops greening. Now I've seen spring over and over, and even if it's the good Lord who has the doing of it, the effort of it tires me out. I think of Him up there with all the thousands and thousands of leaves to unfold and all the trees impatient, waiting their turn."

I took a deep breath and said, "Mrs. Miller, it doesn't seem like Mr. Miller is so happy to have Eleanor home."

"You have to excuse my John. He's had a hard time of it. He's got too much land to handle, even with Tom to help, and no money for a hired hand or a machine that could take over some of the work. Every time I spend a penny, John sees a bit of land getting away from him and resents it something terrible, as if it was an arm or leg he was losing. Then, when Eleanor got so sick, he just thought she wanted to get out of doing her share. If it was her father paying for Eleanor's care instead of the state, Eleanor would never get the help she needs." Mrs. Miller sighed. "Now I'm worried that Tom might go off. His dad is a hard man to work for."

Eleanor returned with a bowl of fat blackberries, and we all sat down to a supper of sliced cold pork roast, fried potatoes, watermelon pickles, blackberries, and sponge cake. I was not allowed to help with the dishes but was sent off with Tom to gather eggs that Mrs. Miller insisted we were to take back with us, though Mr. Miller looked unhappy about that.

When we entered the henhouse, the chickens flew off their nests, their flapping wings creating little whirlwinds of dust and straw. Tom said, "This always used to be Eleanor's job. She loved the chickens. She knew each one by name. She even won some ribbons at the state fair for her pullets." He carefully laid two brown eggs into the basket I was holding.

"Tom," I asked, "when did Eleanor become sick?"

"It was around the time of the deer. Pa never stopped letting Eleanor know things would have been better for the farm if she had been a boy, so she tried hard to help with the work. Eleanor could pitch hay and spread manure and even handle a gun when the rats got too many in the corncrib, but Pa didn't like it. *Kirche, Küche, Kinder.* That's German for 'church, kitchen, children.' Pa says that's all women should tend to. It didn't matter how hard Eleanor tried, she couldn't get a kind word out of Pa.

"Eleanor liked to go off into the woods. She knew all the animals. She'd take a handful of lettuce for the woodchucks and apples for the porcupines, and they'd take them right from her hand. She had a deer she'd leave corn for, and after a while she got that deer tamed. She could get him to come to her by calling in a certain way. I could always tell when she'd seen that deer, because she'd come hurrying back from the woods all excited. When hunting season came and Dad and I went off with our guns, she didn't say anything. She knew we needed the venison. We counted on it to help get us through the winter.

"A couple of days went by, and Dad got glummer and angrier about not getting his deer, and Eleanor watched him. He would help me do the milking; then he'd go off and hunt for an hour or two. By midmorning he'd be back at work empty-handed and mean. The third day Eleanor slipped away in the afternoon and was back at suppertime just as we were sitting down. She walked into the kitchen, carrying the deer rifle, her face all red from crying. 'I got a deer, Papa,' she said. 'You and Tom need to come and dress it out.'

"Dad didn't believe her. 'What kind of joke is that?' he asked, angry at her.

"'It's true,' she said. 'Come and see for yourself.'

"It was true enough, and I knew how she got it. Nothing but wanting to look good in Pa's eyes would have brought her to kill that deer she tamed, but all she got from Pa was 'Not much meat on it.'

"Eleanor just kind of crumbled. She went upstairs into her room and wouldn't come down; she wouldn't say a word to anyone. When a week went by and she still wouldn't talk, Ma and Pa had an argument. Pa said she would get over it, but Ma insisted on calling the doctor. The doctor said she needed help real badly, and so she ended up in the asylum. At first I was worried, but then I figured anyplace was better than here. Now I know it was the right thing to do. She looks happier than I've seen her in a long time. It must not be just the asylum that's doing it. Your people must be good to her."

I told Tom we loved Eleanor. I didn't say anything about Aunt Maude. Hearing the story Tom had told made me feel terrible. I didn't want to believe that someone could be as cruel as Eleanor's father. I was lucky. I missed Mama a lot, and I wasn't happy with Aunt Maude, but I knew Papa loved me

It was the night after our visit to the farm when Mrs. Larter came by. Supper was over, and we all were in the parlor. I was playing piano, and Papa and Eleanor were beside me, singing. Carlie was on the floor, tying her hair ribbon on Promise. She was closest to the door, and when we heard a knock, Carlie ran to see who was there. As Mrs. Larter came into the parlor, I took my hands from the piano keys. Papa and Eleanor, standing side by side, closed their mouths. For just a second no one moved; then everyone got very busy. Carlie showed Mrs. Larter the fine effect of the bow on Promise. I jumped up from the piano bench. Eleanor hurried into the kitchen. Mrs. Larter said, "What a cozy scene that was, Edward," and Papa turned red.

I didn't understand why Eleanor hurried off and why Papa looked so embarrassed. After all, it was only Mrs. Larter, who often used to call on Aunt Maude.

Mrs. Larter said, "I didn't know patients were allowed to be away from the asylum in the evening."

Papa said, "Eleanor has made a great improvement and is hardly considered a patient at this point. However, she has special permission to stay later to keep an eye on the girls while Maude is away."

"I'm sure Maude would appreciate that." Although Mrs. Larter was smiling, there was no smile in her words. "I thought you might be missing Maude's cooking, so I brought some homemade oatmeal cookies for the girls."

"That was very thoughtful of you," Papa said.

"Aunt Maude never baked cookies," Carlie said. "Eleanor always bakes them."

Quickly Papa said, "Carlie, it's past your bedtime. Verna, take your sister upstairs."

From our bedroom window I saw Eleanor slip out the back door and hurry down the path to the asylum. When I got downstairs, Papa was just saying good-bye to Mrs. Larter. He didn't see me, and as the door closed behind Mrs. Larter, I heard him mumble, "Meddling mischief-maker."

SEVEN

Sooner than we expected, Aunt Maude returned. Papa, Eleanor, Carlie, and I were finishing dessert—raspberry ice cream made from wild raspberries Eleanor, Carlie, and I had picked that afternoon. Carlie was telling Papa how we saw polliwogs in the lake.

"They've all got their back legs," she said.

A little shower of road dust flew in the open windows, and we heard the carriage come to a stop at the door. The next thing we knew, Aunt Maude was hurrying into the house, the driver following with her suitcases and boxes. Aunt Maude threw her arms around Carlie and me, smothering us with her familiar smell, part lavender talcum powder and part camphor salve. I suffered the hug, but Carlie wriggled out of it like a cat that won't be held. It was then that Aunt Maude noticed there were four places set for supper.

Eleanor had sprung away from the table, so at first I believe Aunt Maude thought that somehow we knew she was coming and had prepared a place for her, but it was only a moment before she took in the remains of the melting ice cream and the half-empty coffee cup. She turned to Eleanor and, pointing to the dishes, said in a tight voice, "Take those away, and bring me some cold salad and bread and butter and a cup of tea."

"Yes, ma'am." Eleanor made a grab for the dishes like they were trying to get away and fled into the kitchen.

Papa frowned, but he made his voice pleasant. "Welcome home, Maude. I hope everything went well with the house and the new tenants."

"I have decided not to rent again for the time being. The last tenants left the windows open in a rainstorm, and my curtains are ruined. You can't trust strangers."

As we all settled around the table, Aunt Maude said in a sharp voice, "I had a very nice letter from Mrs. Larter, who mentioned that she had stopped by to visit you." With a glance toward the kitchen, Aunt Maude said, "Edward, I can't believe you allowed a servant to sit at the table as though she were a member of the family."

Carlie said, "Eleanor taught us how to make bread and how to whistle with a piece of grass. She caught polliwogs for me at Green Lake. They're going to start their front legs. Eleanor put some in a jar for me, and I can watch them be frogs."

"I can see I was foolish to leave you, but I had not thought that you would have allowed the children to be so much with someone who was not in her right mind."

Papa took off his glasses and began to clean them with his handkerchief, just as he always did when he was angry. I think he did it to give himself time to calm down. Finally he said, "You are not a physician, Maude, and therefore in no position to pronounce whether a person's mind is right or not. In this case you could not be more uninformed."

Eleanor came in with a plate of salad just in time to see Aunt Maude burst into tears. "I don't know why I even bothered to come back," she said. "I see that I am not wanted here."

Papa was on his feet at once, comforting Aunt Maude. "Nonsense, Maude, you know how grateful to you I am. I don't know what we should have done without you. You are tired and hungry from the journey. Eat something, and you will feel much better."

Eleanor quickly set the plate of salad down and hurried into the kitchen. Father had been so busy consoling Aunt Maude that he had not seen the tears in Eleanor's eyes, but Carlie and I had, and now Carlie began to cry.

"You see how that woman upsets the children," Aunt Maude said.

For an answer, Papa closed his mouth into a tight line, and I was sure he was holding in words he knew he ought not to say to Aunt Maude.

After that evening Aunt Maude had two purposes: to show that she could teach us things as well as Eleanor, and to prove that Eleanor was not in her right mind and ought to spend her days in the asylum rather than with us.

The next morning, before Carlie and I could get out the door, Aunt Maude ordered us into the parlor, where we were initiated into the mysteries of the ladylike art of crocheting. The crochet hook was awkward in my hand, and the little loop that it invaded was always too small for the hook or so large that the hook would have nothing to do with it. I gritted my teeth and kept trying, but Carlie grew impatient and began to cry. Aunt Maude quickly excused her, sending her out to play, but I was kept indoors until I had completed a bumpy spiderweb.

I remembered how Mama had taught me to knit doll

clothes, laughing over my mistakes, telling me she had made many more when she learned how to knit. With Mama the knitting had been for the pleasure of being together. With Aunt Maude, teaching was to show who was in charge.

A few days later I was introduced to tatting, which was truly punishment. It was accomplished by the use of numerous small bobbins of thread that were like a dozen untamed puppies that rolled about and tangled their leashes. Carlie hid under her bed with her jar of polliwogs for company or escaped into the yard, but I had to sit still for an hour and watch summer slip away.

Aunt Maude saw that Papa had grown fond of Eleanor, so there was no meanness when he was about, but Papa was gone all day. Aunt Maude didn't pull Eleanor's hair or beat her, though that might have been kinder, for hair would grow back, and bruises heal. This meanness lurked under the cover of kindness like a serpent got up in ruffles and a bonnet.

On an afternoon, soon after Aunt Maude returned, Carlie and I set off for the dairy with the gallon jug on our usual errand to get milk. "Eleanor," Aunt Maude said, "it's such a pleasant afternoon; take your hour off and go along with the girls."

Eleanor was as taken aback as I was, for she had given up her time off, afraid of Aunt Maude's anger. At first she hesitated. "You said I was to make a peach pie for supper, ma'am."

"You'll have plenty of time to do that when you return."

Happily Eleanor set off with us, pausing just outside the door to look about, as if the whole world had been created right then and there just for us. She had something to say about everything she set eyes on. She stopped to show us how each blossom of Queen Anne's lace had a tiny purple flower in the middle of its bloom. A row of milkweed plants grew at the field's edge. The fragrance from their blossoms smelled like the little sachets Mama had made up to put among her handkerchiefs. Eleanor was more practical. "Milkweed makes good eating," she said. "You boil up the young seedpods or give them a fry. Delicious with a big lump of butter." Orange butterflies were hanging on the milkweed blossoms. "Monarchs," Eleanor explained. Carlie was going to catch one, but Eleanor held her back. "If you disturb the dust on their wings, they won't be able to fly."

Not far from us a goldfinch settled on the top of a mullein plant, its feathers gold in the sun. In the midst of the brightness I had a dark thought. Like Mama, Eleanor might soon leave us. Only that morning Eleanor had whispered to us that her doctor said she was well enough to return home at the end of summer.

"Will you be happy to leave the asylum?" I had asked.

"I'll miss you and Carlie a lot, and I have many good friends—not only other patients but some of the attendants. I help the attendants and sometimes even the doctors to talk to the German patients. There are a lot of patients who have come over from the old country and know hardly a word of English. It's a terrible thing when you can't explain yourself. It makes you *ängstlich*; that's German for 'anxious.'" I made Eleanor repeat the word for the penny it would get me.

"If I leave the asylum, I'll have to go home," she said. She sighed. She didn't mention her father, but I was sure she was thinking of him.

After filling the jug and stopping at the barn to admire a calf so new that it could barely stand, we headed home. On the way Eleanor pointed to a large gray bird with black wings and tail. The bird was sitting in a tree, watching some little chickadees that were nervously flitting from branch to branch. "A shrike," she said. "Cruel birds. I saw one catch a little song sparrow and kill it by sticking it on a barbed-wire fence."

Carlie asked, "Did you kill the shrike?"

"Oh, no," Eleanor said. "It is only doing what such birds are supposed to do."

We returned just as Aunt Maude was leaving to join a group of doctors' wives who met each Thursday afternoon. "Don't forget the pie," she told Eleanor.

Eleanor made the peach pie and, as a special treat, sprinkled the crust trimmings with sugar and baked them for Carlie and me to eat. When they came out of the oven, Carlie took the first bite and spit it out. "It's all salty."

I didn't believe her and bit into my own piece. It tasted terrible, as if a whole shaker full of salt had been sprinkled onto it. Eleanor nibbled a bit of the pie and made a face. She reached for the sugar canister and, licking a finger, stuck it into the white powder and tasted it. Her eyes were huge. "It's salt!"

"Why is salt in the sugar canister?" Carlie asked.

Eleanor and I looked at each other. I was sure Aunt Maude had done it on purpose. Eleanor didn't know what to think. She wanted to throw the pie away, but I made her save one piece. Hastily she baked a second pie, this time with the sugar that had been put into the salt canister. When Aunt Maude came home, she sent Eleanor and Carlie and me out to pick some tomatoes from our garden. I pretended to go, but I looked into the kitchen window in time to see Aunt Maude switch the salt and sugar back where they belonged. When I told Eleanor what I had seen, she looked as if I had struck her. "You must have made a mistake," she insisted. "She wouldn't do such a thing." After that she said not another word but moved about silent and thoughtful, speaking only when she learned what I planned to do. "You'd be as bad as she is, Verna." But I didn't care, and Carlie couldn't wait for me to do it.

When it was time for dessert, I handed around the plates, giving Aunt Maude the piece I had saved from the salty pie. Aunt Maude took a forkful and spit it out. "It tastes of salt. It's inedible. Eleanor must have reached into the wrong canister. She is getting more and more absentminded."

Papa took a bite of the second pie. "Why, it's excellent. Whatever can you mean, Maude?"

Carlie and I each took big mouthfuls. "My favorite," Carlie said.

"The best ever." I licked my lips.

Aunt Maude insisted, "Edward, try a piece of my pie."

Papa looked up. "Thank you just the same, Maude. I've had more than I should."

Desperate, she turned to me. "Verna, taste this."

I gritted my teeth and swallowed a small piece. "Delicious," I said with a big grin. Hurriedly I ate a bite of my pie to get rid of the salty taste.

Aunt Maude, looking uncertain, took another small bite and made a face. She reached over and took a piece of my pie and then a piece of Carlie's. Her face became very red, but there was nothing she could say.

After that Carlie and I had only to say "peach pie" when Aunt Maude was out of hearing, and we ended up in fits of giggles, but Eleanor could not see the humor in what had happened. She would not confront Aunt Maude but only asked over and over, "Why would she do such a thing?"

A few days after the peach pie we began making plans for the asylum picnic. Every summer Dr. and Mrs. Thurston held an outdoor gathering for the patients and for all those who worked in the asylum. Entertainment was provided by the patients and staff, and the Thurstons, who often commented on Papa and Eleanor's fine solos in the choir, now asked them to sing a duet.

Mrs. Thurston offered to play the piano while they rehearsed their song, so each evening after the supper dishes were done, Eleanor combed her hair and changed into her one good dress, which she brought to work with her. Before the first visit to the Thurstons' home, Eleanor confided to me that she was nervous. "Even a little frightened, Verna. It's not like I am just going home to the asylum, but right into the home of the superintendent." I noticed as she started off, she lagged a bit behind Papa, like Carlie on her first day of school. Papa strolled along, his hat tipped in a way that showed he was feeling cheerful. You could always tell the way Papa felt by how his hat sat on his head. The Thurstons must have made Eleanor welcome, for on the second night she marched along right beside Papa.

Carlie and I begged to go along, and the third night Papa said we might if we would sit quietly during their rehearsal. He asked Aunt Maude if she would like to go as well, but looking very haughty, Aunt Maude said it was too hot to leave the house.

After the peach pie Aunt Maude had become quiet and said only what was necessary to Eleanor. When Aunt Maude heard that Papa and Eleanor were to sing together at the picnic, you could tell she disapproved, for she wandered about the house surrounded by a sulky cloud of anger that settled over all she did. When Carlie and I left for the Thurstons' with Papa and Eleanor, Aunt Maude's resentment followed us all the way like a snarling dog nipping at our heels.

Though it was early evening, the August heat still hung on so that in the walk from our house to the asylum I felt trickles of perspiration between my shoulder blades and on my forehead. The leaves on the trees had grown dull and dusty; the daisies drooped; the butterflies seemed weary, hardly bothering to flutter their wings. The setting sun was red hot, and it tinted the large white asylum a rosy pink. Inside the building it was cool. Whatever heat managed to get through the thick brick walls stayed up in the high ceilings and left us alone.

After greeting us, Dr. Thurston said he had work to do in his office, and Carlie and I settled quietly on the davenport, nibbling on molasses cookies, while Macduff sat nearby hoping for crumbs. Mrs. Thurston seated herself at the piano and held her hands up in the air, waiting for Eleanor and Papa to stand beside her. I could see that Eleanor was uncomfortable in the Thurstons' sitting room. She stood a little apart from Papa, staring at the floor and clutching her hands together as if they might fly apart, but once the singing began, Eleanor forgot her shyness. The song, "Oh, Promise Me," was sad in a beautiful way. Even Carlie paused in her eating of the cookies to listen, though only for a moment.

After the rehearsal was over, Eleanor went on to her room in the asylum, and Papa and Carlie and I walked back in the soft darkness. Carlie, knowing that at home bed was waiting for her, kept asking Papa questions to make the walk longer. "Why are there shadows from Dr. Thurston's trees when there isn't any sun?"

Papa pointed to the full moon, and that made Carlie ask questions about what kept the moon up in the sky. Her next question made Papa stop and look at her. "Why does Aunt Maude hate Eleanor?"

"Carlie, Aunt Maude doesn't hate Eleanor. I believe she is jealous of Eleanor. Unhappily, Aunt Maude believes love is like a glass of water, just so many sips to go around, when really it's like scooping water from a river. Take as much as you like. The river just fills right up again."

In the distance we could see the lighted windows of our house. For several seconds Carlie thought about what Papa had said, and then, seeing that we were nearly home and bed was coming, she asked, "Why don't moths come out in the daytime?" And no more was said about Eleanor and Aunt Maude.

On the day of the picnic Carlie and I were up with the first light, hanging out the window to be sure there were no rain clouds. Even Aunt Maude looked forward to going, although she couldn't keep from asking Papa,

"Why can't the patients have their own picnic?"

To which Papa replied, "The whole purpose of the picnic, Maude, is to show how much the patients and the staff have in common, not to separate them."

The picnic was held on the front lawn of the asylum. The flower beds had been tidied, the grass cropped to a smooth green carpet, and benches set about to make the grounds into a huge outdoor sitting room. Some of the patients seated on benches were accompanied by attendants. I guessed those were the patients from the back wards and wondered if Eleanor's friend Lucy was there.

Men were pitching horseshoes, the clang against the iron stakes making a ringing noise. A croquet court had been set up, and I saw Louis, the gardener, frowning as someone tramped over a flower bed in search of a wooden ball. Aunt Maude joined Mrs. Larter, their large hats overlapping as they bent toward each other for chattering purposes. Carlie headed for a long table where the asylum cooks were setting out bowls of potato salad, several great hams, pickles, hills of rolls, angel cakes with thick frosting, cherry pies, and jugs of lemonade.

I had pried Carlie away from the food to watch a game of baseball when we heard Eleanor's laugh. A sack race was getting started. It was men against women. Cries went up for the Thurstons, and to our surprise Dr. and Mrs. Thurston appeared to expect the invitation. Mrs. Thurston gathered her skirts and Dr. Thurston took off his jacket, and they both climbed into sacks. Papa followed suit, encouraging Eleanor and tossing sacks to Carlie and me. We waited for the race to start. There were a dozen of us falling and picking ourselves up and toppling over again.

Everyone gathered around to see the Thurstons cheerfully make fools of themselves. Some of the women who stood about had put up parasols against the sun. Aunt Maude was one of them. Carlie and I waved frantically to get her attention, but she was staring at Papa, who was helping Eleanor into her sack. Aunt Maude's face was very red. A moment later the signal was given for the race to begin, and off we went, Carlie trying to keep up with my bigger bounces. I saw that the other racers were holding back so that the Thurstons could win, and they did, to shouts of congratulations. Eleanor came in second for the women. She stood there looking flustered and happy and laughing in a way I had never heard her laugh at our house. For the first time I saw that she was not just *our* Eleanor but Eleanor herself.

When it was time for lunch, Papa spread our blanket on the lawn and sent us after Aunt Maude, but Aunt

Maude would not come. "It's unhealthy to sit on the ground," she said. "Verna, bring me a plate of ham and potato salad and a glass of lemonade."

Because Aunt Maude had the company of Mrs. Larter, who stayed with her on the bench, I thought nothing of it, but Papa scowled. "I believe your aunt has forgotten how to enjoy herself."

After lunch, as we all lay about the lawn, full and sleepy in the sun, the entertainment was announced. A maypole had been set up, and six women in white dresses and with wreaths of flowers in their hair advanced toward the pole and gathered up the ends of six ribbons that had been attached to its top. Around and around they danced as they sang a song about May that didn't make any sense because it was August. I had to cover Carlie with the blanket to keep her from giggling. A patient played "Yankee Doodle Dandy" with a mouth organ, and one of the attendants recited "The Wreck of the Hesperus," which frightened Carlie so much that she was back under the blanket. At last it was the turn of Eleanor and Papa. Eleanor didn't move until her friends gave her a push. As she walked up to join Papa, she kept her eyes on the ground as if she were searching for something. When she reached him, there were cries of encouragement, and after a moment she looked up at Papa, who nodded that they should begin. There was no piano on the lawn to accompany them, but all the rehearsing had helped them to sing together in perfect harmony.

The moment the last note faded away, there was loud applause. Carlie and I stood up and applauded until our hands were sore. Eleanor and Papa bowed to the audience, and Eleanor hurried back to her friends, who threw their arms around her.

A man pulled scarves, and then a rabbit, from a hat. Carlie was sure the rabbit was meant to be hers and was furious at the man for making it disappear. When the picnic was over, we looked for Aunt Maude, but she wasn't there. Papa said, "I saw her leave a little while ago. She must have been tired." There was a worried frown on his face. Carlie and I, bored with sitting still and happy to be let loose, ran home ahead of Papa.

I expected Aunt Maude to be flustered and angry, but she was bustling around, her sleeves rolled up and an apron tied around her waist. She said, "I'm making a lemon sponge dessert for supper tonight. Eleanor never gets it right." Because of the picnic, Eleanor had the day off.

Carlie was wandering around the house, looking on shelves and in cupboards. She complained, "I can't find my polliwogs."

Aunt Maude said, "They were beginning to smell, Carlie, and I was short of canning jars for the peaches. I threw them out."

Carlie shouted, "No, you didn't!"

"Don't contradict me, Carlie. They were dirty, ugly things. I can't think why you would want them."

"They were getting their front legs," Carlie sobbed. She ran outside and began searching around the house. I heard her wailing, and when I went outside, I found her bending over her dead polliwogs, lying like ink stains on the grass. She ran into the house and began kicking Aunt Maude on the shins.

At that moment Papa walked into the house and snatched up Carlie. "Carlie! Stop that! What's gotten into you?"

As Papa carried her up to her room, Carlie was screaming, "She killed my polliwogs."

Papa came downstairs, taking each step carefully, as if the stairs were steep and dangerous. "Maude," he said, "I wonder if I could have a word with you. Verna, I noticed the rose bed hasn't been weeded. That's your job. Go outside and do it right now."

I went out, but the minute the door closed on me, I scrunched down, hardly breathing, under the open kitchen window. Papa was saying, "Maude, I believe you are upset at how close the girls and Eleanor have become. Because Eleanor had given Carlie those polliwogs, you thought to punish her, the Lord knows why, and all you did was upset Carlie. What you did was thoughtless and cruel."

Aunt Maude sounded like she was crying. "I have tried to do my best and be a mother to those girls, but I can see I'm not wanted here."

Papa's voice softened. "Maude, that's not true. Of course you are wanted. I am only pointing out that deeds have consequences, and if you had given a little thought to it, I am sure you would have realized how upset Carlie would be. As for Eleanor, she is a very competent young woman and is trying her best."

"You are letting that woman take my dear dead sister's place."

Papa snapped, "That is unworthy of you, Maude. No one could take Isabel's place, but you must admit that Eleanor has been very good with the children."

"Edward, you may as well know that if that woman comes back into this house, I will leave."

"You can't mean that, Maude."

"I do mean it. I can take care of this house and the girls without any help from her."

There was a long silence. I could not believe Papa

would give in, but he must have felt sorry for Aunt Maude. With a terrible feeling of doom I heard him say, "Well, all things considered, it might be best. I learned today that they think at the asylum that Eleanor is well enough to go home for a long visit. This might be a good time for her to do it. We certainly can't have another scene like the one this afternoon. It's very bad for the girls." I heard Papa's footsteps coming to the door and dashed to the rose bed.

Papa called, "Verna, would you go upstairs and see to your sister?"

Carlie was sitting cross-legged on her bed, her face very red and angry, her eyes flashing. "I hate Aunt Maude. I hope she explodes into a thousand pieces."

I tried to cheer Carlie up by letting her play with my best doll, which I didn't usually do because she always made a mess of the hair when she combed it.

When Papa called us for supper, Carlie refused to come downstairs. "I won't eat her food. She touched it."

"Carlie, don't be stupid. Of course she touched it. How else could she cook it?"

"She touched it with the same hand she used to kill my polliwogs." Carlie was half upset and half enjoying the scene she was making.

Nothing would make her come downstairs, so Papa

had to go up and carry a sullen, silent Carlie down and place her at the table. She sat there with her mouth tightly shut, staring straight ahead, refusing to eat. Aunt Maude coaxed her. Papa ordered her. Still she refused. Finally, Papa shrugged and said, "Well, one meal more or less won't make any difference."

After supper Carlie followed me out of the house. "Let's go to Green Lake and get some polliwogs," Carlie said.

"We're not allowed to go there unless someone is with us," I said.

"Well, Eleanor can take us tomorrow."

I should never have told Carlie when she was already unhappy, but it was all I could think about. I was feeling almost like Mama had died all over again. So it just came out. "Eleanor won't be back tomorrow," I said.

"What do you mean?"

"I overheard Papa and Aunt Maude talking. Aunt Maude said she wouldn't stay if Eleanor kept on working here. Papa said Aunt Maude should stay."

"Eleanor's never coming back?"

I shook my head. "She's going home to the farm."

"I'm going to starve myself to death, because I'll never eat anything unless Eleanor cooks it."

I was sure Carlie liked food too much to give it

up—even for Eleanor—but I had an idea. "Listen," I said, "if you really refuse to eat, I'll promise to sneak food to you. If Papa thinks you're starving, he's sure to get Eleanor back."

"You promise you'll get me stuff to eat?"

"I promise." I was thinking only about bringing Eleanor back. I wasn't thinking about what my plan might do to Eleanor.

EIGHT

༄

The next morning Carlie refused her breakfast. Aunt Maude looked hurt. She took away Carlie's plate of scrambled eggs and stirred up a batch of pancakes. Pancakes were Carlie's favorite, but Carlie shook her head and closed her mouth tighter than ever.

Papa said, "Just ignore her, Maude. She's bound to eat when she gets hungry."

It was easy to snatch some of the leftover pancakes and put them in my pocket. Carlie complained, "They have fuzz from your pocket and no syrup." But she ate them.

At dinnertime Aunt Maude said, "I've made deviled eggs for you, Carlie, the way you like them with chopped pickle."

Carlie wouldn't pick up a fork. She just sat there.

Even when Aunt Maude put a plate of Carlie's favorite coconut macaroons on the table, Carlie just looked at them for a long minute and then looked away. Later, eating the deviled egg and the macaroons I had sneaked up to her, Carlie asked, "How soon will Eleanor come back?"

"Papa has to get worried first," I said.

At suppertime Papa was angry. "This has gone far enough, Carlie. You have made your point, and this foolish behavior must stop right now. It's endangering your health, and I won't have it."

Carlie slunk down in her chair and wouldn't look at Papa.

"Do you hear me, young lady?"

I was afraid Carlie would give in, but she only stuck out her chin and said, "I won't eat until Eleanor comes back."

Aunt Maude jumped up and left the table. Papa said, "You see how unhappy you have made your aunt Maude, Carlie?"

"I don't care," Carlie said. "She made me unhappy."

"Carlie," Papa said, "Eleanor has gone home."

Carlie said, "She'll come back if you ask her."

Papa stood up and threw his napkin on the table. "Go up to your room, young lady."

Carlie slipped off her chair and climbed the stairs,

stomping one foot after the other. Papa went into the kitchen after Aunt Maude. I grabbed some ham and bread and ran upstairs to Carlie. My sister snatched the food and gulped it down so fast she nearly choked. Then she grinned. "This morning, while Aunt Maude was in her bedroom, I sneaked some dried apple slices from the pantry and ate them."

After that it was a game. I never thought about our doing anything wrong. I only wanted Eleanor back. It wasn't fair that first we had lost our mother and now Eleanor was gone. Besides, I was sure Eleanor would be happier with us than she would be with her father.

At mealtimes Carlie sat at the table refusing food, shaking her head, her mouth pressed shut, her fists clenched. Aunt Maude's voice would start out normal. Soon it would get shrill, and her face red. Papa would calm Aunt Maude, and then he would talk to Carlie, explaining in a reasonable voice that she must eat for her health. After a while Papa would grow impatient and lose his temper. He would send Carlie to her room. By the end of the third day Papa looked worried, and I began to feel guilty about sneaking food to Carlie. It was easy to do. It was the end of August, and the asylum gardens were full of food: tomatoes, peas, and carrots. Carlie had to eat them uncooked, but she was so hungry, she didn't care. I picked wild blackberries and took leftovers from the icebox and a piece of cake from the pantry. Aunt Maude asked why I wore the same dress three days in a row. She never suspected that it was because it had large pockets.

Although she wasn't supposed to be eating, Carlie was playing just as she usually did, following me around, chasing rabbits, making hollyhock dolls. Papa watched Carlie with a puzzled look on his face. The evening of the third day he called me aside. "Verna, are you giving food to Caroline?"

I had guessed this moment would come, but I hadn't known what I would do. The idea of lying to Papa was terrible, but I told myself that a lie wasn't so wrong if it was for Eleanor's sake. Papa hadn't been at the farm to see how unhappy Eleanor's father made her. I thought about having to suffer through years of Aunt Maude. "No," I told Papa, "I haven't given her any food."

"Is she getting food somewhere else?"

"No. I'm with her all the time."

"Listen," I told Carlie afterward, "if you aren't eating, you should be weak. You shouldn't be running around. You should stay in our room."

"I want to go outside."

"Well, you can't. Papa is suspicious."

It helped that on the next day it rained. Carlie refused breakfast and dinner and lay on her bed looking sad, which had more to do with the rain and having to stay inside than with being hungry because at dinner I sneaked part of my sandwich and a handful of brown sugar from the bin. Brown sugar was Carlie's favorite, but she had trouble getting so much down all at once.

When Papa called Carlie for supper that evening, Carlie wouldn't come downstairs. "She's not feeling well," I said. "She just lies there on the bed."

I followed him up the stairs. Carlie was pale. She really did look sick. "Caroline, this has gone far enough," he said. "You are ruining your health. Give it up and come downstairs. Aunt Maude will make you whatever you like to eat."

Carlie shook her head. No matter what Papa said to her, she wouldn't answer him but just clamped her mouth shut. Tears were running down her cheeks. I knew she wasn't hungry and began to worry. Papa stopped being angry and looked upset. The minute he started down the stairway, Carlie jumped up, snatched the potty from under the bed, and was sick into it.

When she was finished, she told me, "It was the brown sugar. I was afraid Papa would see it coming up and know I was eating."

Downstairs we could hear Papa having a conversation with Aunt Maude, and Aunt Maude being angry about something, but Papa just kept on talking in a low voice, and after a bit Aunt Maude stopped answering back.

The next morning, when Carlie refused to come down to breakfast, Papa said to Aunt Maude, "I'm going out in the buggy."

"Where are you going, Papa?" I asked. Papa just glowered at me. Aunt Maude stalked into the kitchen and began banging pans. When the screen door slammed shut after Papa, I ran upstairs.

"Carlie, we won. I'm quite sure Papa is going after Eleanor."

"Not *we*, *me*, Verna. I ate all the raw carrots and peas and the brown sugar. You had real meals."

"If I hadn't given you food, it would never have worked. And it was my idea. Anyhow, if Eleanor is coming back, what difference does it make?"

We knelt on Carlie's bed and watched out the window. We knew it would take a couple of hours before Papa got back, but we didn't move. The rain had stopped. Outside, the hot sun made steam come up from the puddles and the wet paths. The trunks of the trees were a shiny black from the rain, and in the garden the drowned delphiniums lay on the ground. People who had stayed inside to keep out of the rain were hurrying from the asylum to their outdoor work.

The time dragged. I had to go down to dinner when Aunt Maude called. She sat right there and watched me the whole time, so I couldn't put anything in my pockets. She was very angry. "Your father is much mistaken if he believes it is wise to give in to the whims of a six-year-old."

I was certain now that Eleanor was coming, and if Eleanor came, I was pretty sure Aunt Maude would leave. I believed the same carriage that carried Eleanor to us would carry Aunt Maude away, as if there were room in the house for just one of them and Eleanor would be the one to stay. Papa had said Eleanor was better now, so she wouldn't need to go back to the asylum in the evenings. She could sleep in Aunt Maude's room after Aunt Maude left.

I was thinking abut how different the house would be with Eleanor there when the carriage pulled up and Eleanor walked into the house behind Papa. She was carrying a small suitcase. Eleanor looked scared. She looked as if she had been made to come when she didn't want to. "Hello, Miss Maude," Eleanor said. Aunt Maude didn't say anything.

"Verna, go upstairs and bring down your sister," Papa said. "Tell her Eleanor is here."

Carlie and I hugged each other, and then we hurried

down the stairs. Carlie looked like she was going to run to Eleanor, but Papa got hold of her. "Carlie, I have explained everything to Eleanor. She agrees with me that you have been very foolish. She will see that you eat some food, and then she will tell you herself that you must stop this behavior."

Tomato soup and cheese sandwiches were on the table. Carlie sat down and opened her mouth like a little bird waiting for worms. Eleanor sat next to her and began to feed her spoonfuls of soup. Carlie swallowed as fast as Eleanor could get the spoon to her mouth.

Papa looked very solemn. Aunt Maude watched without saying a word. When Carlie reached for a cheese sandwich and began to stuff it into her mouth, Aunt Maude glared at Eleanor. "You have ruined these children," she said.

Eleanor cringed as if she had been slapped. Papa said, "Maude, you had better keep quiet."

"I have no intention of keeping quiet. This woman with her odd ideas and sick ways has bewitched these children. She has been an evil influence. You can see for yourself she would let Caroline starve in order to worm her way back into this house. Mrs. Larter and several of the women have spoken about the impropriety of her working here. Even the asylum sent her away."

"She went home because she was well, Maude. As for the gossiping women, that is beyond contempt."

Eleanor looked small and frightened, just the way she had looked when she first came to us. She gave a great sigh. "I'm sorry if it was my fault that Carlie's stopped eating."

When she saw how miserable Eleanor looked, Carlie wouldn't let her take the blame. "It wasn't your fault. I *was* eating."

Nothing was turning out as I had planned. I had counted on everything being better if only Eleanor would come back, and now here she was and everyone was still unhappy. With my sneaking food to Carlie and lying to Papa, I had made things worse and not better. I felt the truth coming like a fast train, and I couldn't stop it. "I gave her food to eat," I said. "I gave her vegetables and ham and macaroons."

Aunt Maude grabbed at my words. "That only proves what I have been saying," she said. "She turned those children into thieves."

At that Eleanor hid her face in her hands.

Papa looked very sad and said, "I am sorry to say, Maude, that it is you who brought the girls to this. You thought that if they loved Eleanor, they would stop loving their mother." He turned to Eleanor. "It was very kind of you to come, Eleanor. You have no reason to blame yourself. We would appreciate it if you could stay on for a while until things straighten out."

Eleanor nodded her head that she would do as Papa asked. Aunt Maude made a sort of strangling sound as if she were choking on words. Eleanor looked at Aunt Maude as if Aunt Maude were the shrike ready to swoop down and stick her to a barbed-wire fence.

Papa said he wanted to talk with me. I followed him into his study, my feet dragging, my heart pounding. "Verna, your deceit has been a great disappointment to me. What you did yourself is bad enough, but much more troubling is your encouraging your little sister to join you in your skullduggery."

Skullduggery! I cringed. I had never heard the word before, but it had an evil sound. "Papa," I pleaded, "Aunt Maude deceived you too." I told Papa about the pie made with salt.

"Aunt Maude must answer for her own behavior, Verna, but can't you see how much she longs to be loved and accepted by you and Carlie? Your aunt Maude is an unhappy woman, made more unhappy by your coldness to her. If she had your love instead of your rudeness, there would have been no need for salty pies. I am afraid that in trying to bring Eleanor back, you not only have been a poor example for your sister but have made things more difficult for Eleanor. You saw how unhappy she was to be thrust into all this unpleasantness."

I was crying so hard that Papa took pity on me and, ceasing his terrible words, sent me to my room. Every word he had said was true. I lay on my bed, wishing I were dead, while Carlie tried to comfort me. "Eleanor's here," she said. "So everything is all right."

I wouldn't be comforted, for I had made trouble for Eleanor and lied to Papa. Eleanor had had to stand there and listen to the awful things Aunt Maude said about her, and Papa had told me I had been a disappointment to him. I didn't see how things could be worse.

NINE

Although Carlie was eating again, she had not forgiven Aunt Maude. She stayed away from Aunt Maude, and Aunt Maude noticed it. I saw her look longingly at Carlie the way a hungry person peers in the window of a grocer's. I knew I hadn't been kind to her. Maybe I wouldn't be a disappointment to Papa anymore if I tried to love her the way she wanted. But I didn't know how to begin with the loving. When I tried, Aunt Maude always managed to say something that shut my love up inside me again, like the afternoon she showed us a picture of herself and our mother when they were our age. "Caroline looks so much like Isabel when she was young," she said. "My little sister was always the beauty in the family. I'm afraid I was more like you, Verna." I shuddered, horrified at the thought that in any way I was like Aunt Maude.

At any rate, Aunt Maude didn't seem to care what I felt. The one she wanted to love her was Carlie. To win Carlie's favor, Aunt Maude spent what little money she had on gifts for my sister: a small parasol, a doll whose eyes opened and shut. When Carlie said she wanted a petticoat with ruffles, Aunt Maude spent hours shirring and hemming, only to have Carlie complain that the ruffles scratched her legs. The more Aunt Maude reached for Carlie, the farther away Carlie ran. It was Eleanor my sister wanted to be with, but Eleanor, afraid of Aunt Maude's anger and jealousy, made it a point to be busy with her tasks.

One afternoon I was playing dolls with Carlie, making a tea party in the backyard from dandelion water and cookies we stole from the pantry, but I was much too old for that kind of thing, and I was bored.

"Let's find Dr. Thurston," I suggested. Dr. Thurston walked among his trees after dinner every day. I liked to get him to tell me what country each tree came from, and then I would go home and make up stories about the foreign lands.

"His stories are boring," Carlie said. "Why can't we go to Green Lake and get more polliwogs?"

"No, Carlie," I said. "Papa warned us against going there. Anyhow, Green Lake isn't any fun without Eleanor."

I didn't think it was fair that I had to spend every day taking care of my little sister and doing all the stupid things she wanted to do, so I left Carlie with her dolls and tea parties and escaped to the asylum grounds to hunt out Dr. Thurston. He seemed glad to see me and showed me a twisty willow tree from Japan.

"In Japan people will sometimes keep a tree small by trimming its roots and branches," he said. "I've seen a willow that was three hundred years old and only a foot high."

When I got home, I began writing a story of a girl who lived in a forest of those little trees. There were tiny animals too, and the girl had to be careful where she stepped. Because she was so big, her shadow made acres and acres of shade, and on hot days all the little animals followed her around to escape the sun. I was writing about how hard it was for her to get enough to eat when all she had were potatoes the size of peas and peas so small you couldn't see them. I was lost in the story when I heard Aunt Maude call to me.

"It's time to clean up for supper. Where is Carlie?" she asked.

"I don't know," I said. My conscience stung me when

I realized I hadn't thought to look for her.

"You are supposed to be keeping an eye on your little sister, Verna."

That was true, and I felt guilty. "I'll find her," I said. I searched the usual places. She wasn't in the secret cave she had made under the back steps or in the yard, hidden in the bushes, waiting for rabbits to come and nibble the parsley in the garden. I was going next door to the Schmidts', where Mrs. Schmidt often gave us a hard candy to suck on and one for our pockets, when Aunt Maude called to me.

She was in the kitchen with Eleanor, frightened looks on both their faces. Aunt Maude pointed to the trash basket. A little pile of canned peaches lay there. "Carlie has emptied out a canning jar," she said. We all guessed what Carlie was after.

"She's gone to get polliwogs." I was the one who said it. Eleanor threw off her apron and started for the door. I was right behind her.

In a voice that sounded as if it were having a hard time getting out, Aunt Maude said, "I'll get your father."

All I could think of was the mud that sucked at you like hands pulling you down. You had to walk through the mud to get to where the polliwogs were. Eleanor with her strong, long legs had no trouble, but she had always warned us against wading there.

The two of us ran in the direction of the lake, Eleanor far ahead of me. The path was wooded and curved one way and then another, so you didn't see the lake until you came right upon it. I ran until I was out of breath, and the pain in my side was like a knife slicing into me. I was mad at Aunt Maude for throwing away the polliwogs, but I was just as mad at myself for leaving Carlie alone. I promised God everything I could think of, if only He would keep my sister safe. I would play dolls with her. I would never answer Aunt Maude back. I would give up desserts. I would give my coat with the fur collar to some poor child.

Eleanor was far ahead of me. I heard Carlie's cries before I saw the lake. Eleanor was wading into the water. All I could see of Carlie was her head and shoulders. Eleanor plucked her out of the mud and carried her onto the shore, Carlie clutching Eleanor about the neck. When Eleanor tried to put her down, Carlie clung to her and wouldn't let go. It was only when Papa arrived, running and out of breath, that Carlie allowed herself to be untwined from Eleanor. In a second she was in Papa's arms. Papa stood there hugging Carlie as if holding her were the only thing that kept the world together.

"I lost the jar in the mud trying to get the polliwogs,"

Carlie said, her voice muffled against Papa's chest. "Aunt Maude will scold me."

"She won't scold you, Carlie, but you were very wrong to go to the lake by yourself. You must promise me never to do such a thing again."

Carlie's head nodded up and down. Papa turned to Eleanor. "Thank the Lord you got here in time. We are once again indebted to you."

We made a little parade walking back to our house: Eleanor, me, and Papa carrying Carlie. Word had gotten out that Carlie was missing, and a crowd had gathered around our house: neighbors and gardeners and employees who had been at the asylum when Aunt Maude came for Papa. There was a cheer when we appeared with Carlie. Aunt Maude ran toward us.

"Thank heavens. This is the last straw. Look what has come of that woman dragging those children to the lake."

Eleanor looked stricken, like Aunt Maude's words were a slap, as if she believed Aunt Maude that it really was all her fault and she was responsible for every bad thing that ever happened in the whole wide world.

When Papa saw the expression on Eleanor's face, he put Carlie down. "Maude, Eleanor saved Caroline's life. We have much to thank her for. Eleanor, would you kindly take the child inside and get her cleaned up? Verna, you can give Eleanor a hand. Maude, I want to have a word with you."

The people stood together talking for a few minutes, and then, as we went inside, they left. Carlie was pleased with all the attention she had received and submitted happily to the bath Eleanor gave her, but Eleanor had no words at all. She wouldn't answer Carlie's questions. She was all closed up, like the morning glories that grew on the porch railing and shut themselves up every night so that they looked wilted and dead.

Even from upstairs we could hear the shrillness of Aunt Maude's voice, but not what she was saying. It was only later, when Aunt Maude did not appear for supper, that Papa explained. "Girls, your aunt Maude is packing her things. She is going to her home. I am sure we will miss her, but we can't expect her to continue to sacrifice her liberty to care for us."

Papa's solemn tone kept Carlie silent for once. I was quiet too, for fear of saying something that would keep Aunt Maude from leaving. Eleanor's hands were shaking when she came in from the kitchen with slices of blackberry pie for us. I had thought that Eleanor would be happy at the news of Aunt Maude leaving, but she didn't look happy. She looked defeated, as if she had been running a long race and had lost.

I pushed my slice of blackberry pie away. Papa stared at me. "What's the matter, Verna? Carlie is safe. There is nothing to worry about, and you were a great help today."

"I promised," I said.

"Promised? Promised who?"

"God. I said I'd give up desserts if God let Carlie be all right."

Papa put down his fork and stared at me. He put his hand over mine. "Verna, that's not the way God works. You can't bribe Him."

I hadn't actually thought of it as a bribe, but after Papa explained, I felt foolish. How could you bribe someone who had the whole world? I dug into my pie.

"But you were right to ask Him," Papa said, smiling. "It was the asking that counted, not the bribe."

I remember exactly what happened next. Carlie finished her pie and got up to look in the mirror over the sideboard to see if her tongue was purple. Papa took out his pocket watch to check the time we had finished supper. He liked to know how long everything took; time is the only thing Papa is selfish about. I was looking out the open dining room window at a chipmunk sitting up chattering to itself. Eleanor came in to clear the table.

She was watchful and cautious, as if the plates were dangerous and might fly off the table and attack her.

Aunt Maude made such a bustle as she marched into the room, we all stopped what we were doing and looked at her. "I suppose I may spend the night?" she said. "You won't turn me out."

Papa sprang up and flung his napkin onto the table. "Maude, that was uncalled for. I have told you how much I have valued your care of Verna and Carlie. I only thought since your house was available to you, you might be more comfortable there. I'm afraid the children are a little too much for you."

"Too much for me, but not too much for her." She glared at Eleanor. "I'm surprised you have not considered what people will say after I leave."

Eleanor made a noise, a sort of whimper, like a rabbit cornered by a fox. Carlie ran over and grabbed Eleanor's hand as if we were going to play some game and she had chosen sides.

Papa said, "There will be no occasion for evil gossip, Maude. I have explained to Eleanor that it would be inappropriate for her to stay on here. She understands that." He turned to Eleanor. "Get your things, Eleanor, and I'll take you back to the farm right now. I see no reason why you should have to stay here and submit to such unwarranted attacks."

Eleanor seemed confused. She looked around help-lessly. Papa said, "Verna, get Eleanor's things for her."

Eleanor didn't even say good-bye to us but followed Papa to the buggy as if she were a naughty child who was being sent to her room. Once he had settled Eleanor in the buggy, Papa came back into the house and into the front hall, where Aunt Maude was. His words snapped like a whip. "Maude," Papa said, "you should be ashamed of yourself. I only hope your cruel and thoughtless words have not undone the help the asylum has given Eleanor." Aunt Maude had a shocked look on her face, as if one step more and she would fall into a great pit that had opened right at her feet. Papa turned on his heel and walked out of the house.

Carlie and I sat on the steps of the front porch watch-ing as the buggy carried Eleanor away.

"What if she doesn't come back?" Carlie said. She was hanging on to me, afraid I would disappear as well.

"She will," I said, but I wasn't so sure. Eleanor hadn't gone away as if she were coming back. I thought about what it would be like for Eleanor to return home, blam-ing herself. I wished Papa had seen what Eleanor's father was like. He wouldn't be sending her back. I didn't understand why Papa cared about what busybodies said.

I didn't understand why Eleanor couldn't stay with us. At last Aunt Maude was going, but Eleanor was leaving as well. It wasn't fair.

We both heard the sound at the same time. At first we were afraid to go inside, but after a minute I made myself get up and walk through the door. Carlie followed me, hanging on to my skirt. Aunt Maude was in the parlor, sitting on a chair, her hands covering her face, her suitcases scattered about the floor. She was crying in great gulps. Carlie scrambled onto Aunt Maude's lap and threw her arms around her. A minute before, when we were on the porch, I had hated Aunt Maude. Now, seeing how miserable she was, I tried very hard to forgive her, but my forgiveness was thin and grudging and cold as ice water.

TEN

After Aunt Maude left, Mrs. Luth, another patient from the asylum, came to keep house and care for us. Though Carlie and I pleaded with Papa to bring Eleanor back, Papa kept insisting that since Aunt Maude wasn't there anymore, it wouldn't be proper for a young woman like Eleanor to be working at our house. Mrs. Luth wasn't anything like Eleanor. She was older than Aunt Maude and Papa. She had a blank face, as if she were waiting for an expression to come and settle there. She spoke in a whispery voice, and then just when she had to, but she was kindly and baked us molasses cookies. She never minded if Carlie made tents outdoors with the sheets or if I read all day, neglecting the chores Papa had assigned me. She would even do the chores for me, but she wasn't Eleanor. Eleanor was at the farm. When we went to the chapel on Sundays and Eleanor wasn't there, Papa still sang, but he didn't sound like his heart was in it.

The leaves on the trees were turning yellow, and the fields were purple with wild asters. The potatoes had been harvested, cornstalks filled the asylum silos, and in the glasshouses Louis was potting up chrysanthemums that gave off a sharp, sour, spicy smell.

Sad letters came from Aunt Maude with their hopeful hints. If we needed her, she could return at any time. Wouldn't it be helpful if she came to show Mrs. Luth how everything should be done? Carlie begged some chrysanthemums from Louis and put them in an envelope she had me address to Aunt Maude.

"They'll be squashed," I said.

"Aunt Maude will like them anyhow," Carlie said. I knew Carlie was right.

Summer ended, and it was time for school. Carlie and I both had new straw hats and pinafores. The schoolhouse was a mile and a half from the asylum, an easy walk when we had a warm September sun to travel along with us. In the winter horses would take us on a sleigh. As we walked along the country road, we passed a farmhouse where three horses stood close together in a field. They were always in the same place and seemed to watch for us, following us with their eyes, their long necks turning as we passed by. Somehow, even though I missed Eleanor so badly, the patient horses made me feel better. They were always there.

After the farmhouse we came to an apple orchard where a few red apples still hung on the trees. Beyond the orchard was a field planted with winter wheat. Though the other fields were brown stubble, this one was spring green and hopeful. Beyond it were some woods. We caught sight of the deer bounding among the trees, and once a red fox with a bushy tail darted across our path. After the woods was the farmhouse where our teacher, Miss Long, boarded.

The schoolhouse was red brick with gray smudges where we sharpened our pencils on the bricks. In the back were a woodshed, a privy, and a well for drinking water. All twelve grades were taught in one large room. The kindergartners sat up in the front of the schoolroom, and the older students in the back, although some of the older boys were helping with the harvest and would be slow in returning to school. On the wall behind Miss Long's desk was the blackboard and, above it, pictures of President Washington and President Lincoln with the American flag between them. There was a stove in the middle of the room, but the weather was still warm, and the stove hadn't been lighted.

Miss Long wasn't much older than the high school students. With her serious expression, her hair pinned up, and her long skirts, she looked like a young girl playing at dress-up. I felt sorry for Miss Long, always having to live in someone else's house. Once when I stayed inside to clean the blackboard and she was outside settling an argument between two boys, I saw a list on her desk labeled RULES FOR TEACHERS:

You must be home by 8:00 P.M.
You will not marry during the term
    of your contract.
You are not to keep company with men.
You may not loiter in ice cream stores.
You may not dress in bright colors.
You must wear at least two petticoats.

I thought of Eleanor's word *eingeschlossen*, shut in. With such rules to bother her, it was no wonder Miss Long's expression was solemn.

Carlie and the other first graders were called up to the front of the room in the morning for their spelling recitation; then it was the second graders' turn, and so on through the grades. I found it difficult to concentrate on learning my Latin declensions and the Constitution when I had to sit all day long listening to recitations of things I already knew. The classroom was warm and stuffy, and it was hard not to fall asleep. There was no clock, but I could tell from the shadows that moved from Miss Long's desk to the firewood box to the water pail and dipper how close it was to the end of the school day.

When I complained to Papa, he sat me down at the dining room table every night and, placing his pocket watch on the table, gave an hour to drilling me on my Latin and history. He took time with Carlie as well, going over her lessons and admiring her pictures of houses with the sun shining on them. He knew we missed Eleanor and tried to make up for it, but I could see from the way he kept glancing at his watch that he longed to be in his study working on *The Closed Door*.

I had looked forward to school. Though I loved my sister, I longed to be friends with someone my own age, so I was happy to see that besides me there were two other girls in seventh grade, Norma and Alice. There was also a boy, John Walters. John's family lived on the farm with the horses, and he sometimes joined up with Carlie and me in the morning, but when we got close to the school, he ran ahead so that the other boys wouldn't see him walking with girls. He reminded me of his horses, for he had a lock of blond hair that fell over his forehead like a forelock and a quiet, patient way about him. He didn't say much, but he listened hard. When I told him how I liked his horses, he said one day he might let me ride one. John and his father helped with the asylum's corn harvest every year, working in the fields with the patients.

At first Norma and Alice shared gossip with me about the other students—how Sarah Clark and William Rush kissed on a dare and how Mary Lee put lemon juice on her hair and sat in the sun to make it more yellow—but they wanted gossip from me in return. They had heard where I lived, and they coaxed me for stories about the patients. People like John and his father who had worked at the asylum knew what the asylum was really like, but others who had nothing to do with it imagined all kinds of strange things.

Norma asked, "Do you have anything to do with the patients?"

"Yes," I said.

"Is the asylum a dangerous place to live?" Alice wanted to know.

"No."

"What if the patients escaped?" Norma asked.

"Most of them walk around wherever they please."

The girls were disappointed when I had no horror stories. They didn't believe me when I said you couldn't always tell patients from people who just worked at the asylum. Alice asked, "Are you sure your father is a doctor and not a patient?"

At first I had eaten my lunch with Norma and Alice, but now they took their lunch pails and ate with some sixth graders. I saw them looking at me and whispering. I sat under a tree by myself and made up stories that I was sure Norma and Alice would like to hear, stories about wild men and women at the asylum who jumped out from behind the trees and chased you. If I told such stories, they would be eager to be friends with me, but if I told lies like that, how could I face Louis or Mrs. Luth or all the other people in the asylum? Most of all, how could I have faced Eleanor? Eleanor was always on my mind, a singing bird hidden high in a treetop.

One afternoon Carlie ran over to me at recess time, crying. "Someone pinned a note on my back, and I can't reach it. Take it off." She wriggled as if a poisonous bug had latched onto her.

Printed on the paper were the words "I BELONG IN THE CRAZY HOUSE." I unpinned the paper, my hands shaking with anger. Carlie looked at the paper. "What does it say? I haven't had those words in spelling."

"Never mind. Who pinned it on you?" She pointed to Albert, an eighth grader. He was one of the boys who often had to sit up on the front benches with the little children for throwing spitballs or making rude remarks when someone had to be excused to go outdoors to the privy.

Albert towered over me, but I didn't care. I marched up to him and stuck the note under his nose. "Did you put this on my sister?"

"What if I did?" Albert grinned and looked around to see if his wit had been appreciated.

John, who was watching, said, "You leave those girls alone."

Albert looked with a smirk at the others on the playground who had gathered around us. "You telling me what to do?"

"You bet I am." John moved in closer to Albert. Albert pushed him away. John pushed back. In a minute they were rolling around on the ground, pounding on each other. Miss Long appeared with a pail of water, which she threw on them. The rolling around stopped, and they both sat up, wiping the water from their eyes with their fists.

Miss Long said, "Dry yourselves off, and then go and sit with the kindergartners, where the two of you belong. I expected better things of you, John."

Hurriedly I said, "It wasn't John's fault. Albert pinned this on the back of my little sister." I held out the evil paper.

Miss Long glanced at it. "That was very wrong of Albert, but John must learn that ungentlemanly behavior will settle nothing."

As usual, John ignored us as we left school, but Carlie and I waited for him at his farm. As he turned in to his path, I said, "I'm sorry you got in trouble over us."

"That's all right. I've been wanting to get after Albert for a long time."

"You said you would let me ride one of your horses."

He grinned. "You're putting me to a lot of trouble today. All right, come on while I drop off my books, and then I'll saddle one up."

"What about me?" Carlie asked. "The paper was pinned to *my* back."

"You can get up on the horse to see what it's like, but you're too small to take one out for a ride."

A couple of collies that had been sitting on the back porch of the farmhouse raced to greet John, their tongues hanging out, their tails beating the air. He pushed his way past them and held open the screen to the back door, motioning us in. Mrs. Walters had been canning, and the kitchen was hot and steamy. She paused from putting jars of pears into a kettle of boiling water and wiped the perspiration from her face with the dish towel. "Come on in. You must be the girls from the asylum. John told me about you. John, give the girls a piece of pie and a glass of milk. I can't leave this kettle while it's on the boil." She gave the pears a critical look. "These pears are full of worms, and digging the worms out has spoiled the look of them. I hear you've got some fine orchards over at the asylum."

Before I could answer, Mrs. Walters started talking again. I guessed why John didn't say much. Probably he never got the chance.

"I've got a friend whose farm is next to the Millers'. Their Eleanor worked for you. Mrs. Miller told me you lost your mother. I don't know anything sadder than that. I suppose you got someone to look after you now, but it isn't like your real mother. John, not the apple pie. That's left over from last night's supper. Look in the pantry. There's a lemon meringue just baked this morning."

I looked for a way to say something, but Mrs. Walters kept talking, so I followed John and Carlie's example and just worked on the pie, which was delicious.

Mrs. Walters was saying, "It's too bad about Eleanor Miller. My friend says Eleanor is in a bad way again. She doesn't say a word to anyone, just sits staring into space. Her ma wants her to go back to the asylum, but her dad won't let her. He blames the people at the asylum. He says they ruined her."

I choked on my pie. Eleanor was sick again, and no one had said anything to us.

Carlie stopped eating. Her face crumpled, and she began to cry.

Mrs. Walter looked surprised. "I guess I talked out of turn. I thought you would know about Eleanor."

John hadn't been paying attention to his mother's words, but now he could see she had upset us, and looking for a way to get us outside, he said, "I'll pick up the saddle and take you out to the horses."

Mrs. Walters ladled the boiling syrup into the jars of pears. She warned, "If you let them get up on a horse, be sure it's Star. She's the most gentle."

"Thanks very much," I said. "I think we'd better go home. Maybe we could come back some other time."

I took Carlie's hand and started for the door.

John looked hurt. He followed us to the road. "It was probably something Ma said. She talks so much, she's bound to get around to saying something she shouldn't."

"No, it's not your mother's fault. It's just that when Eleanor left us, she was nearly all better. I've got to find out what happened." I snatched Carlie's hand and began running. Over my shoulder I called, "I'll see you tomorrow."

Carlie and I couldn't wait for Papa to get home from the asylum but met him on his way. He looked from me to Carlie. "What's the matter, girls?"

I repeated Mrs. Walters's story. Papa was half angry, half worried. "She must come back to the asylum," he said. "She mustn't stay there with that impossible father of hers." Papa stopped himself. "I shouldn't have spoken of her father in that way. I was only thinking aloud."

"You have to go and get Eleanor," I said.

"No, that wouldn't be appropriate."

"Please, Papa," Carlie said. "Eleanor's sick. John's mama said so."

"Carlie, a doctor can't go storming into a home and take away a patient, and I'm afraid it would amount to that."

"Then what will happen?" I pleaded, "We have to do something."

"I'll speak to her doctor. In the meantime let's hope her family will realize what is needed."

But Eleanor's father thought the asylum had ruined Eleanor. He would never let her come back. I decided that if Papa would not go get Eleanor, I would.

ELEVEN

அௌஸ

Papa didn't leave for the asylum until after Carlie and I left for school. I started off with Carlie as usual, knowing that if I said I wasn't feeling well, Papa would return during the day to check on me; besides, I didn't want to have to tell him another lie. Carlie and I were nearly at the schoolhouse when I stopped suddenly and clutched my stomach.

Carlie stared at me. "What's the matter?"

"I have a stomachache. You go ahead. I'm going to rest a little, and then I'm going back home."

"I'll stay with you until you're better."

"No. Just tell the teacher I don't feel well."

Carlie looked puzzled. "You were all right until just now."

"Stomachaches can come on suddenly. Just go

ahead and let me be."

"I don't believe you."

"Carlie, don't argue. You'll be late for school."

"You don't look like you're sick. You look like you're going to do something and you don't want to tell me what it is."

"If you must know, I'm going to see what's wrong with Eleanor. I'll tell you all about it when I get home."

"I'm going too."

"No, you are not."

Carlie stuck her chin out. "Yes, I am."

I saw that there was no use arguing with her. "All right, but you have to swear to do just what I say." Before I even finished my sentence, Carlie was running down the road on the way to Eleanor's farm.

By eleven o'clock we had covered the nine miles and were turning onto the Millers' road. The farm was familiar from our visit, but now it had a hushed look. The windows and doors of the farmhouse were shut. It was fall, and everything had stopped growing; even the animals were silent. We stood at the gate. Carlie pulled at me, but I had thought only this far. I didn't know what to do next. When I didn't move, Carlie ran up to the back door and called Eleanor's name. The door opened, and Mrs. Miller stood there staring at us, her hand over her mouth as if she were afraid she would cry out. She looked around quickly and then pulled us inside.

Mrs. Miller's sleeves were rolled up, and her hands and arms were covered with flour. There was a dusting of flour on her cheeks. I could smell bread baking. She tossed back a lock of hair that had fallen over her forehead so she wouldn't have to touch her hair with her floury hands.

"Where is Eleanor?" Carlie asked.

Though there didn't seem to be anyone else in the house, Mrs. Miller looked around before she answered, "Eleanor's upstairs in her room." In a worried voice she said, "Tell me what Eleanor did."

"What do you mean?" I asked.

"How come your dad fired her from her job?"

"My father didn't fire her."

"He fired Aunt Maude," Carlie said.

She looked from me to Carlie and back. "You'd better sit down and explain to me what happened."

I told her how Aunt Maude was jealous of Eleanor and was always after her and how Eleanor had saved Carlie from drowning and how after he sent Aunt Maude away, Papa said it wouldn't be proper for Eleanor to work for us. "But that wasn't because he didn't want her to," I said.

"It was what the busybodies would say."

"I tried to tell my husband it was something like that," Mrs. Miller said, "but he wouldn't listen. Eleanor was looking so unhappy that he insisted she must have done something very wrong to get let out of her job, something like stealing or being bad to you little ones. He says the asylum has made her crazy, and he won't let her go back. He's after her all the time to tell what she did, but she just keeps quiet. Once he shook her so hard, I was afraid she would fly apart, but she won't say a word, only stays in her room. He's worn her down. She's right back to being like she was. I pleaded with him to let her go back to the asylum to see the doctors, but he refuses."

"She can come back with us," Carlie said.

"She'd never be able to walk that far. She's weak and wasting away. Everything's two sizes too large for her."

Tom had come in the room and was standing there, listening. "I can hitch up the wagon and take her," he said. "We got to do something, Ma, or she'll just curl up and disappear."

"Your dad would have the hide off you," Mrs. Miller said.

"I don't care. I'm as big as he is, and I told him if he knocks me around anymore, I'll take off. He knows I mean it and he needs me."

As Mrs. Miller stood there trying to make up her mind, Carlie started for the stairway, with me right behind her. We had no trouble finding Eleanor's room. The door was open, and Eleanor was sitting on the floor in a corner. At least I thought it was Eleanor. It didn't look like her. Instead of being pinned into a neat bun, this woman's blond hair straggled down to her shoulders in tangles and wisps. Her dress hung on her like an empty pillowcase, and the buttons were mismatched with the buttonholes. She wore no shoes, and strangest of all, her hands, which had always been red from work, were white as if they were dead.

Carlie and I ran over to her and tried to put our arms around her, but she didn't seem to recognize us and cowered even farther into her corner. Tom and Mrs. Miller stood at the door. There were tears running down Mrs. Miller's face, streaking the fine powder of flour. Tom went over and picked Eleanor up as if she were a bag of dry leaves. We hurried downstairs. Tom left his sister on a chair and ran out to hitch the horses to the wagon. Mrs. Miller put shoes and stockings on Eleanor and tried to do something with her hair. Then she hurried to the window to watch for Mr. Miller.

Tom carried Eleanor out to the wagon. Carlie and I climbed in on either side of her. Mrs. Miller stood by, fretting. "I hope I'm doing the right thing. I don't know what Mr. Miller will say." To me she said, "You tell your daddy to take good care of my Eleanor."

We were all so busy with Eleanor, none of us noticed Mr. Miller striding up and snatching the horses' reins. "Where do you think you're going? What are you two doing on my farm? I thought you got rid of my girl."

"No, sir," I said. "She saved my sister's life. We want her back."

"Well, you can't have her. She's not some stray cat you let out and take in when you please. Anyhow, the way she is, she's no good to anyone. Tom, you put that wagon back."

Mr. Miller was a fierce sight. His face was red, and his mouth twisted into an ugly shape. Carlie scooted closer to me, and I felt Eleanor trembling. I grabbed on to one of her hands and held it tight.

Tom looked at his dad. "Better let go of the reins," he said.

Mr. Miller reached up and tried to yank Tom off the wagon, but Tom wouldn't be yanked. He just held on. His dad said, "I'm going to beat the hide off you."

Tom wasn't riled or angry, just icy cold. "You've given me the last beating I'm going to get. You lay a finger on me, and I take off. Any job I find will be better than this one. Let's see if you can handle this farm by yourself."

"I don't think you should talk to your pa like that, Tom," Mrs. Miller said.

"It's the only talk he understands," Tom said. His dad had let go of the reins, and now Tom got the horses started up. I was afraid his father would lunge at him, but Mr. Miller just stood there looking as if he'd like to slam his fist down on the whole lot of us. The wagon moved slowly at first and then faster as Tom urged the horses on. I was sure Mr. Miller would come after us, but when I looked around, he was still standing there, his arms at his sides, his fists doubled up.

We were quiet in the wagon, as if we had used up all our strength and now all we had to do was just keep going. I hoped Eleanor would brighten up once we got away from the farm, but she didn't. When we finally reached the asylum, I wasn't sure what to do.

Tom said, "You'd better go and get your papa."

I couldn't move, afraid of what Papa would say. I was worrying about what we had done. What if the asylum wouldn't take Eleanor back? I knew there was a proper way to get people in, but I didn't know what it was.

"You wait here," I told Tom, "and keep Carlie with you." With a last look at Eleanor I marched into the asylum and up the stairway to where the Thurstons lived.

Mrs. Thurston was arranging some flowers in a vase. She said, "Why, Verna, what a nice surprise. Did you come to pay me a call?"

"No, ma'am. I brought Eleanor Miller. She's outside in the Millers' wagon."

Mrs. Thurston put down the flowers. "You'd better tell me about it, Verna."

As I told the story, Mrs. Thurston looked more and more worried. "It's not proper to bring the child back here if it's against her father's wishes."

"But her mother wants her to be here," I said. "Just come and see her for yourself."

Mrs. Thurston looked doubtful, but she followed me down the stairway. As soon as she saw Eleanor, Mrs. Thurston sent for Dr. Thurston. Minutes later Dr. Thurston was leading Eleanor inside.

Mrs. Thurston said, "Tom, you'd better stay and have a talk with Dr. Thurston." She turned to us. "Girls, you go on home. I'll explain everything to your father."

Carlie and I were too nervous to eat the egg salad sandwiches that Mrs. Luth fixed for us. We sat on the porch steps all afternoon, watching for Papa. "Will Eleanor get better?" Carlie asked.

"She got better before," I said, but I wasn't sure how many chances you got.

We had sweaters on, but the clouds had slid over the sun, and I had goose bumps on my arms. Our lawn was losing its green, and the maples along the road were showing red leaves. I sat there with Carlie, thinking of all the different kinds of scoldings we might get from Papa. We had been absent from school. We had gone to Eleanor's farm without permission. We had helped Tom bring Eleanor here after her father said she couldn't come. I had walked right into the Thurstons' apartment and bothered Mrs. Thurston. The waiting got worse and worse. Half of me wanted Papa to be late, and half of me wanted Papa to come so we could get the scolding over with.

It was nearly suppertime when we saw Papa walking home from the asylum. Usually we ran to meet him, but now we sat still, watching to see what Papa's hat would look like. Most of the time he wore his hat a little pushed back from his forehead, but when he was really angry, he put it on square like he had slammed it down on his forehead. I saw it was slammed down.

Papa stood looking at us. Carlie never could stand a silence. She said, "Hello, Papa."

Papa sat down between us on the steps and took my hand and Carlie's hand in his. "Are you angry, Papa?" I asked.

"Yes," he said, "very angry."

I waited for what would come next.

"I am angry at myself for being such a poor doctor and, worse, a poor friend. You two are better psychiatrists than I am. Certainly you have been better friends to Eleanor. I cannot say it was right to spirit her away from her home, but before he went back, I had a long talk with Tom, who told me Eleanor's mother wishes it. There is no question that Eleanor should be here, where she can have the help she needs. I should have gone to see Eleanor myself, but I believed we had caused her unhappiness, and I imagined she needed a vacation from us. I had not taken her father into account. After Aunt Maude's harsh ways, her father's cruel scoldings were too much for her."

"Can Eleanor come back and take care of us?" Carlie asked.

Papa said, "Eleanor is not well enough."

"Can we see Eleanor?" Carlie asked.

"When she is more herself," Papa said.

"When will that be?"

"Not for a while, Carlie."

Papa had spared me, but I knew that I had been lucky, for I had taken a very big chance. I told myself that I should just be patient and wait until Papa told me when I could see Eleanor, but I knew I would not be patient. I was sure I could help her, sure I knew her better than anyone else. Hadn't I been the one to rescue her?

TWELVE

❧❦❧

I t was Louis who told me where I would find Eleanor. "In the afternoon, if the weather's decent, they take her out to the little locked garden and let her sit for an hour so she can have a bit of fresh air. She's all alone and looks so sadlike. I guess she'd be happy to see a friend."

The next afternoon when I got home from school, I went to find Eleanor. Carlie was busy furnishing a crate box for her clothespin dolls: scraps of cloth for curtains, acorn caps for dishes, and bits of twig for furniture. She hardly looked up when I said I was going out for a while.

I came to the locked garden along a narrow path that twisted among birches and maples. The October trees were polka-dotted with red and yellow. The last of the milkweed seeds were floating on their tiny umbrellas. The only bird sound was the raspy call of a blue jay. The whole outdoors looked like a room that had just got a good cleaning with everything put away.

Eleanor was huddled on a bench in a far corner of the garden, humming to herself. Even with Eleanor there, the garden looked deserted. The roses had finished their blooming, and the fountain had been shut off against the first freeze. She had gathered branches to make a kind of shelter, so you had to look twice among the twigs and dried leaves to see her. In spite of her heavy sweater she looked thin. Her pale hair had escaped its knot and lay in tendrils about her shoulders. She had a wary look, like some small animal that had made a hiding place for itself.

She was so strange and so different from my Eleanor that I didn't know what to say to her. She was like a seedling you start inside too early, which makes it all leggy and pale and when you plant it outdoors it just wilts. I gathered some of the brightly colored maple leaves that had fallen and held them out to her. I was crying. After a minute she left her shelter and came over to me. She reached through the iron railing and took the leaves with one hand; with the other she wiped the tears from my cheeks. I grasped her hand, and she didn't pull away.

"Eleanor, Carlie and I made the sugar cookies you taught us how to bake," I began. But Eleanor said nothing. I tried again. "When the leaves came down, I found the robin's nest in the maple tree. You know, near where we found the pretty blue egg."

Eleanor wouldn't say so much as a word. When I was little, if something was bothering me, my mama used to tell me a story to cheer me. Climbing into the world of the story, I would forget all about what had made me unhappy. So Carlie wouldn't be suspicious, I had taken my notebook with me when I left as if I were going off to write stories. Now I opened it. "I'll read to you," I said. Eleanor nodded.

I read the story of the girl in the forest of small trees.

"It's your turn now," I said. "You tell me a story."

Eleanor was quiet for a long time, and I was afraid she wouldn't say anything. Finally, in a voice so soft I could hardly hear her, she said, "My story is just the opposite of yours. It's about a girl in a forest where the trees and the animals and all the other people are large, but she is very small, like an ant or a tiny beetle. She is fine as long as she stays quiet and no one sees her, but she knows if she makes a movement or a sound, someone will notice her and make trouble for her."

Eleanor wouldn't say anything more. When I saw the

attendant coming to unlock the gate and take Eleanor back to the asylum, I slipped away.

I asked Papa how Eleanor was that evening. In a worried voice he said, "I'm afraid she hasn't spoken a word to anyone."

I wanted to say, "She talked to me," but I thought of the small girl hiding in the large forest. Maybe Eleanor was hiding; maybe she didn't want to see anyone but me. The truth was that I was pleased that I was the only one to whom Eleanor talked. I liked having a secret with Eleanor.

Each afternoon, in fine weather, Eleanor was allowed in the locked garden for an hour. If I hurried home from school, I would be in time to visit her. At first Carlie was suspicious, but about the same time, John surprised her with a rabbit from his farm, and Papa said she might keep it. She named it Surprise. After that Carlie was as anxious as I was to get home. Leaving her telling Surprise what had happened that day in school, I hurried to the garden.

I always brought something for Eleanor: a deserted goldfinch nest woven cleverly out of a twist of fibers, the transparent skin a snake had shed, a branch of witch hazel with its spidery yellow blossoms, the last of the fall flowers, reminding Eleanor how once we had looked for these things together. Eleanor examined each gift closely, smiling as she took it in her hands, but she told no more stories. She was silent except for the singing. She would not sing if she saw me, but if I was very quiet as I approached the locked garden, I would hear her. She sang quietly, songs and hymns and tunes I had never heard. The singing there in the deserted garden was strange, like a summer songbird singing from a winter tree. It was as if Eleanor believed words had become too dangerous to use, as if they were all sharp and saw-edged and hard, and only words softened by music were safe.

At first Eleanor would stop singing as soon as she saw me. If I asked her to go on, she shook her head. But after a few visits she kept on with the singing even after she saw me coming.

I wanted Eleanor to be my secret, so I hadn't said anything to Papa about my visits until one evening at the supper table when Carlie asked, "When are we going to see Eleanor?"

Papa wasn't Eleanor's doctor. When we had asked why, Papa explained to us, "A patient feels more comfortable talking to someone she doesn't know well." Now Papa told Carlie, "From what her doctor says, I'm afraid it will be a while. She still isn't talking." Papa sounded very sad. "She is in the ward for very sick people."

I couldn't bear to think of Eleanor shut up in the ward where there weren't any pretty things, no flowers or white tablecloths, just people like her friend Lucy. Papa had to know that Eleanor wasn't as sick as he thought. I blurted out, "Eleanor is singing."

Papa looked at me in surprise. "What do you mean, 'singing'?" he asked.

"When the weather is good, Eleanor is in the locked garden. I see her there nearly every day. She doesn't say words but sings them, lots of them."

Carlie was furious. "I hate you, Verna. You sneaked off to see Eleanor and never took me."

"Eleanor is shy," I said. "People make her nervous."

"I'm not people," Carlie said. "I'm Caroline."

It was true that Eleanor was shy, but it was also true that I had been unfair to keep her for myself. I knew she would have welcomed Carlie.

Papa looked puzzled. "I'll have to discuss this with Dr. Thurston. Let's hope it's a good sign."

Carlie would not wait. After school the next afternoon she wouldn't let me out of her sight. When I set off for the locked garden, Carlie was with me hugging Surprise. While I had been taken aback and even a little frightened when I first saw Eleanor, Carlie ran right to her, pushing the startled rabbit through the iron railing. "Here. You can hold Surprise."

Eleanor took the squirming rabbit, and petting it, she sang until it settled down in her lap. Carlie giggled. "It's just a rabbit," she said. "It's not a baby." But Eleanor kept on with her lullabies.

That night Papa said, "I told Eleanor's doctor about her singing, Verna. He said that was very important. It gave him an idea."

"What idea?" I asked, but Papa wouldn't say. Still, I felt proud that my telling about the singing might help Eleanor.

Overnight October went backward from fall to summer. It was so warm, we didn't need sweaters. Little by little Eleanor began to talk with us, just a word or two at the beginning, then more words. One afternoon, when Carlie and I were at the locked garden chattering on to Eleanor about school, Carlie said, "Last week when it was cold, Miss Long fired up the stove, and Albert brought in red pepper and put it on the hot stove, and it made everyone sneeze."

Eleanor actually laughed, and we laughed with her, until we all were laughing together. By the end of October you could hardly stop Eleanor from talking. It was as if she had been filling up with words until they overflowed and poured out of her.

The days were growing cold. In November there were only a few warm enough for Eleanor to sit outside. It was nearly Thanksgiving and the first warm day after a cold spell. The sun was shining, but there was a light dusting of snow in the garden that made it look like it had been painted over with white. Eleanor was looking for us, a smile lighting her face. "I'm to teach singing to the patients," she said. "The patients are to have their own choir. We'll practice every day and give performances for the whole hospital. I can pick any songs I want. I asked if some of the patients from the back wards could be part of the choir. I know I could get them to sing. My time will be after supper. Every night. One of the attendants plays piano, and she'll play for us. Your papa came to talk with me. He said he would help."

I could see the old Eleanor. It was like the game of peekaboo Mama used to play with Carlie when she was a baby. Mama would put her hands over her face to make Carlie think she had disappeared. Suddenly she would take her hands away, and Carlie would laugh with relief. It was what I wanted to do, to laugh out loud with relief because Eleanor was there again.

The trees shed their leaves, and only the evergreen bushes and the pine and hemlock trees filled up the emptiness of the November sky. In the mornings the grass stood stiff and white with frost. Eleanor grew busy and no longer went to the locked garden. Mrs. Thurston told us the new patients' choir was a great success. "I love to stand out in the hall and hear them, Verna. The whole asylum seems filled with music. It lifts me right off my feet. You and Carlie must come and hear the choir for yourselves, and afterward Eleanor will be our guest for tea."

It was Carlie's first visit to the asylum and to the Thurstons' home. She anguished over what she would wear. "When will I have my skirts as long as yours, Verna? I hate the way my white stockings stick out from under my skirt like two of Papa's pipe cleaners. Verna, let me borrow your blue hair ribbon. I put mine on Surprise. If Mrs. Thurston makes me drink tea, I'll throw up. Will we have cookies?"

There was cocoa for us instead of tea, and lots of cookies. Eleanor was there with good news. "I'm not just a patient anymore. They have given me a job teaching music. Even some of the patients in the back wards come to my class. My old friend Lucy Anster can come. She used to need someone with her every minute or she would poke herself with a knitting needle or a knife or anything she could get her hands on to hurt herself. She has scars all over her body. But she's a lot better now, and they're letting her sing with us. She's French Canadian, and we're getting her to teach us French songs.

"And there is more," Eleanor said. "Besides teaching music, I'll be an attendant, helping to care for the patients, and I'll sleep in the attendants' dormitory. I'll have a regular wage."

"Why can't you come back and take care of us?" Carlie asked.

Eleanor blushed. "It wouldn't be right," she said.

"What do you mean?" Carlie insisted.

Before Eleanor could answer, Mrs. Thurston said, "I'm sure that Eleanor would love to return to you, Caroline, but it wouldn't be proper for an unmarried young woman to live without a chaperone in the home of a widower."

"What's *chaperone*?" Carlie asked, and I saw her lips move practicing the word so she could get a penny from Papa.

"It's a kind of protector," Mrs. Thurston said. She handed Carlie the plate of cookies, trying to stop the questions, but Carlie wouldn't be stopped.

"Protect her from what?" I kicked Carlie under the tea table, and she gave me a fierce look. "Why did you kick me?"

Eleanor had been growing more uncomfortable.

Finally she said, "I have to go now, but I'll see you Sunday. I'm going to be singing in the church choir again."

On our way home Carlie said, "I still don't understand why Eleanor can't come and live with us."

"Oh, Carlie, don't you see? It's because of Papa. Papa isn't married anymore. Neither is Eleanor. People like Mrs. Larter would gossip if they saw Eleanor living in our house."

"If Eleanor and Papa got married, would it be all right?"

"Yes, but they aren't going to."

"How do you know? Why can't we make them?"

"You can't make people get married."

"I'm going to ask Papa at supper if he won't marry Eleanor, and I'm getting a penny from Papa for *chaperone*."

Carlie didn't have a chance to ask Papa or get her penny. We had just sat down at the supper table when a wagon pulled up in front of the house. We all recognized it. It was the wagon that had taken us to visit the farm and had brought Eleanor back to the asylum. Carlie and I jumped up from the table, expecting to greet Tom, but it wasn't Tom who had come on the wagon. It was Mr. Miller. He hurried up the walk as if we were going to pull it out from under him before he got to the end of it. Carlie greeted him, but he brushed past us without so much as a glance. "You the doctor?" he said to Papa.

"I'm Dr. Martin. I don't believe I have had the pleasure."

"There's no pleasure. I'm John Miller, Eleanor's dad. Your girls here will tell you who I am. I come to find out what's going on with my daughter."

My heart felt like someone had given it a terrible punch. I didn't want Mr. Miller to have anything to do with Eleanor.

Papa said, "You should make an appointment with Dr. Thurston, who is Eleanor's doctor at the asylum, Mr. Miller. We are friends of Eleanor, but I have no professional relationship with her."

In a snarly voice Mr. Miller said, "What kind of relationship do you have? She worked here, didn't she? You must have talked my boy into sneaking her away from our farm against my wishes."

Did that mean Mr. Miller was here to take Eleanor back? I knew what that would do to Eleanor, and I resolved to do whatever I must to keep her here.

Papa kept his voice calm. "Eleanor was very sick. Mrs. Miller and Tom thought she should be here, and the doctors agreed. Dr. Thurston explained all that to you and Mrs. Miller. You gave Dr. Thurston permission for Eleanor to be here."

"He said he'd go to court if I didn't. That's all changed. Eleanor's not sick anymore. I just saw a letter Eleanor wrote to my wife, and in it Eleanor says she's working for the asylum now, teaching singing. If she's so sick, what's she doing working? If she's well, she can be back at the farm, helping out her mother."

"I believe the doctor feels she would be better off here. The asylum is very pleased with Eleanor's work. Certainly Eleanor is of age and able to make that decision for herself."

"What's age got to do with it? She'll do what I say. I'm her father. I'm not going to have her work here for nothing. I'm going to take her back with me."

"She's not working for nothing. She is receiving a fair wage, and it's up to her to decide if she wishes to go back with you. Now, if you have said all you want to say, I would like to return to my supper."

I could see from the stubborn, angry expression on Mr. Miller's face that all this talk wasn't changing his mind. It was up to me. I slipped out the back door determined to get to Dr. Thurston before Mr. Miller did and make him promise to keep Eleanor from having to go home. I could have found the shortcut to the asylum among the trees with my eyes closed. As I hurried into the asylum, I could see Mr. Miller's wagon coming down the road. I had only seconds. I flew up the stairway to the Thurstons'. They were at the supper table with its neat white linen cloth, its pretty china dishes, and the beets melting red into the chicken gravy.

As soon as they saw me, they jumped up from the table. "Verna, what is it?" Mrs. Thurston asked.

I took a deep breath. "It's Mr. Miller. He wants to take Eleanor back, and we can't let him."

Dr. Thurston said, "I hope that Eleanor will not want to go back with her father. But it's up to her to decide what she wishes to do."

"He's a bully," I said. "He'll make her."

"We won't let him take Eleanor against her will, Verna, but the decision will have to be hers."

We heard footsteps on the stairway. I knew who it was, but I didn't know how to stop him. The receptionist hurried into the room with Mr. Miller right behind her. "I'm sorry, Dr. Thurston," the receptionist said. "I told this gentleman you were at supper, but he wouldn't listen to me."

"That's quite all right, Ethyl. Will you kindly go to the sitting room where Eleanor Miller is rehearsing the choir and ask her if she will come here?"

Mr. Miller glowered at me. "So you sneaked over here to warn them," he said.

Since that was just what I had done, I didn't see how I could deny it, but my coming didn't seem to be doing any good. Why wasn't Dr. Thurston sending Mr. Miller away?

He took a step toward Dr. Thurston. "Let me tell you," he said, "I'm here to take Eleanor home, and no one is going to stop me."

"The only person who could stop you," Dr. Thurston said, "is Eleanor herself."

I crossed all my fingers, but I didn't have a lot of hope. I remembered how Eleanor had given in to her father when he wanted her wages. I remembered the story of the deer.

We could hear Eleanor's voice and the voices of the patients singing and then silence as Ethyl brought in Eleanor. Eleanor was smiling as she entered the Thurstons' sitting room, but the moment she saw her father, the smile disappeared and her face closed in. It was just what I was afraid of. Eleanor wouldn't stand up to her father.

"Eleanor, I come to take you home. You go and get your things."

For a moment Eleanor was quiet, and then she turned to Dr. Thurston and asked, "Do I have to go?" She wasn't doing right off what her father said. For the first time I had a little hope.

Dr. Thurston said, "No, indeed you do not. The

decision is entirely up to you."

"Don't listen to him," Mr. Miller said. "He's got nothing to say about it. It's between you and me. Now do as I say."

My heart sank as I saw that Eleanor was trembling. If she gave in and went home, I was afraid she would end up again on the back wards with patients like Lucy Anster once had been. I was desperately trying to think of something I could do to save Eleanor, and then I remembered how pleased she had been that her singing class was helping Lucy. Now it had to be Lucy's turn to help Eleanor. Without letting myself think about what I was doing, I slipped out of the room and down the stairs to the ward on the first floor, knocking to get the entrance unlocked and telling the attendant, "Dr. Thurston has asked me to bring Lucy up to the Thurstons' apartment."

The attendant looked puzzled. "I don't know. Lucy doesn't have privileges. She's not supposed to be outside the ward."

"It's perfectly all right," I lied. "Dr. Thurston said I should bring her."

Reluctantly the attendant agreed. "I'll have to come with Lucy."

Lucy had a worn-out look, like Carlie's favorite doll that she had loved nearly to death. The attendant held one of Lucy's hands. I took the other hand and shuddered as I saw the scars. "Lucy," I said, "there's a man who wants to take Eleanor away from the asylum. You have to help Eleanor. She helped you, didn't she?"

Lucy nodded.

"All right then—tell Eleanor you need her and that she shouldn't go away."

I had never done anything so hard as walking into the Thurstons' dining room with Lucy. Everyone stopped talking and stared at me until I wanted to hide under the table. Dr. Thurston said, "Young lady, what do you think you are doing?"

Surprise made Dr. Thurston's voice harsh. I had never heard him use that tone of voice before, and its harshness made me realize how foolishly I had acted. Lucy was also alarmed by Dr. Thurston's anger. She pulled away from me and the attendant. Before any one of us could stop her, she reached over to the dining room table and snatched one of the knives that the Thurstons had been using to peel their fruit. I was horrified to see her point it at her arm.

Dr. Thurston said, "Put that down, Lucy." He stepped forward and was going to grab for the knife, but Lucy said, "If you come any closer, I'll stab myself." Dr. Thurston stopped.

We all stood there afraid to move.

Eleanor said to Lucy, "Remember that song we were singing in rehearsal this evening, the one about the moon, 'Au clair de la lune'? It's your favorite."

After a long moment when no one seemed to breathe, Lucy nodded.

"Let's sing it now for everyone." Eleanor began to sing. After a moment Lucy joined her. It was amazing how sweet Lucy's voice was. It didn't match what we were seeing at all. As Lucy sang with Eleanor, Eleanor reached for the knife that Lucy was holding. Lucy gave it to her. I began to breathe again, and Mrs. Thurston, who had sprung up when Lucy picked up the knife, sank down onto her chair. When the song was finished, Eleanor said to Lucy, "We'll go downstairs now." To her father, who looked like he couldn't get out of the asylum fast enough, Eleanor said, "Don't wait for me, Papa. I won't be going home with you."

I could hardly believe what I was hearing. Eleanor was standing up to her father.

Before he left, Mr. Miller said, "That's the kind of crazy people you let my girl spend her time with. She's just wasting her life."

Dr. Thurston said, "A month ago, Mr. Miller, Lucy was locked in a small room. She could not even have a mattress because she would tear out the stuffing and try to choke herself. Now, because of your daughter, Lucy is able to move about freely in her ward. I blame myself for what happened this evening. She was alarmed to find herself in strange surroundings, and worse, I spoke harshly to her. I am confident that she will gradually do better. As for Eleanor, Mr. Miller, she is going to be an attendant, and perhaps will one day even be a nurse."

Mr. Miller headed for the door. "You're all crazy here," he said. He stamped down the stairway.

Dr. Thurston turned at once to me. "Verna, things have turned out well this evening, but you took a great risk. Lucy might have injured herself."

I heard Papa's voice and his steps on the stairway. What would Papa say about my foolishness? I had just gone ahead and acted without thinking. I'd wanted to help Eleanor, but I'd put Lucy in danger. I looked at Dr. Thurston. He said, "You had no right to take a chance with someone else's life, Verna, but if you are sure you have learned your lesson, there will be no need to mention this little incident to your father."

THIRTEEN

cᴐⓖⓞ

The last of the leaves had long since disappeared in the November rainstorms, leaving vacant spaces of sky among Dr. Thurston's tree branches. Wagons passed our house, carrying load after load of coal to feed the asylum's giant furnaces. The locked garden had all but disappeared in the snow. We were so bundled on our way to school that we could hardly move, and the horses on John's farm wore robes of ermine.

Mrs. Luth was nice enough, helping us bake Christmas cookies and even knitting a scarf for each of us as a present, but you couldn't really talk with her like you could with Eleanor, and Papa was busy with *The Closed Door*.

It was the week after Christmas when Carlie said, "I've got an idea. Let's have Eleanor come for dinner.

Then she and Papa could sing together." I guessed what she was thinking. It was what I was beginning to think too. Maybe it wasn't proper for Eleanor to live with us because Papa was a widower. But suppose he and Eleanor got married; then Eleanor would be here all the time. "You ask," Carlie said.

My chance came when Papa had a visit from a famous psychiatrist who had come to see the asylum especially to meet Papa. Papa brought Dr. Magnum home. It was snowing out, and they arrived with little hats of white on top of their own hats. Dr. Magnum was a small, busy man with black chin whiskers like the Thurstons' Scotch terrier. Papa carried him off to his study as if he were something precious, a bit of gold or an expensive diamond. Mrs. Luth brought them many cups of coffee, and Carlie and I could hear Dr. Magnum's high, sharp terrier voice yipping and then Papa's deeper voice like a German shepherd barking. The yipping and barking went on for over an hour, and at last Dr. Magnum and Papa emerged from the study. Dr. Magnum shook our hands and yipped some pleasant words at us, making his chin whiskers go up and down.

After he left, Papa said, "Well, that was most gratifying. Dr. Magnum has read my articles, and he came all this way to tell me that he believes in my theory of mental illness." Papa was all puffed up and grinning.

At once I pounced. "Papa, can we invite a friend

to have dinner with us?"

Papa's mind had followed the terrier out the door, and he had hardly heard what I asked of him. "Whatever you like, Verna. Now you must excuse me. Dr. Magnum has given me some excellent ideas for the book. Go out and play. I must have quiet."

"But Papa, it's getting dark and it's snowing out," Carlie said.

"Anyhow, it's time for supper," I said.

"Yes, so it is. Tell Mrs. Luth I will have my supper in my study."

Papa closed the door to his study behind him. I ran for pen and ink.

"Tell Eleanor to come right away," Carlie said, "before Papa asks who's coming."

"Sunday afternoon is the only time Eleanor has off, so it will have to be next Sunday." Carefully, with Carlie looking over my shoulder, I wrote the letter.

January 23, 1901

Dear Eleanor,

    We would like to invite you to have dinner with us next Sunday. You could come home with us after church.

Sincerely,

Verna and Carlie

"Mrs. Luth," I asked, "could Carlie and I have supper a little later tonight? We have an emergency letter we have to take to the asylum for Papa. Papa is having his supper in his study, and you could leave ours in the oven."

Nothing in the world bothered Mrs. Luth. She never asked questions. Now all she said was: "It'll be in the oven."

We looked to be sure Papa was still in his study, and then, after flinging on our coats and hats and tugging on our boots, we ran along the snowy path from one lighted house to the next. The snow stuck to our eyelashes and crept into our boots. We made footprints up the stairway of the asylum and left the note for Eleanor in the office. "You'll be sure she gets it?" Carlie said.

The receptionist sighed and said, "You can watch me put it in her mailbox yourself."

On the way home Carlie asked, "Should we invite a minister?"

"A minister? What do you mean?"

"Well, if we want them to get married, you have to have a minister."

"Carlie, for heaven's sake. It takes time for people to decide if they want to get married, and then you have to plan the wedding and everything."

The next evening Papa came home with an envelope addressed to me. I tore it open and found a note from Eleanor saying she would be glad to have dinner with us. Without thinking, I said, "She's coming," and danced Carlie around.

"What is this all about, Verna?" Papa asked.

"Eleanor is coming for dinner on Sunday."

"Whatever do you mean?"

"We asked you last night just before supper if we could have a friend, and you said yes. Eleanor is a friend."

Papa looked very serious. "Verna, you will have to write her again and explain that there was a mistake. It is very inappropriate to invite a young woman to dinner into a home where there is no wife."

Carlie's face scrunched up and turned red. I said, "Papa, it would be rude to write her not to come. We already invited her, and she said yes."

Papa thought for a minute. "Mrs. Luth is not even here on Sundays, so there will be no one to make a dinner."

Carlie said, "She leaves cold things for us in the icebox."

"That is hardly a company dinner, Carlie," Papa said.

"We'll make a special dinner for her ourselves," I said. "I know how to cook. Eleanor let me cook with her all the time, and Aunt Maude left a lot of her recipes."

Papa said, "You have done a foolish thing, girls. We will leave it for now, but I must consider how it can best be remedied."

I didn't want to think about any remedies. Eleanor was coming. I was sure once Papa and Eleanor were at the same table, everything would be fine.

On Saturday I coaxed Mrs. Luth into baking a cake for Sunday, and Carlie and I went off to the glasshouse to beg Louis for flowers for the table. Sunday morning Carlie and I were up before light. "What did Mrs. Luth leave for our dinner?" Carlie asked.

I opened the icebox and picked up the covers of the china dishes. "Hard-boiled eggs, salad, and cold chicken," I said. "Cold chicken's too plain, but we can't have something hot because it has to be ready when we get home from church. Papa gets cross when he has to wait to eat." I thumbed through Aunt Maude's recipes. "Here's one for Fowl à la Mayonnaise. That sounds a lot better than cold chicken. It's just cooked chicken on lettuce covered with mayonnaise, and there's a recipe for the mayonnaise. You set the table, Carlie, and remember, knives and spoons on the right and forks and napkins on the left."

The recipe for the mayonnaise sounded simple. I cracked two eggs and let the slippery whites fall into one bowl and the yolks into another bowl. I poured out six tablespoons of salad oil and four tablespoons of vinegar. It said to add the oil and vinegar *very* gradually to the egg yolks while beating them. I found the whisk and started beating the eggs and pouring in the oil and vinegar, but no matter how hard I beat or how slowly I poured, the mayonnaise curdled like sour milk.

Carlie was watching me. "Ugh," she said. "It's all lumps."

"I can *see* that," I snapped. "Go and put the plates out and leave me alone."

I threw the ugly sauce away and started over with our last two eggs. When the lumps began to appear, tears fell into the mess. Lumps weren't romantic. Papa would notice the lumps right away, and it would spoil everything. Carlie came over with the strainer. I looked at her and grinned. After the straining, the mayonnaise still had a few lumps, but you hardly noticed them, and the creamy sauce looked pretty over the chicken, which I arranged on the lettuce and put back into the icebox to keep cool. In the living room I spread some sheet music on the piano so I could play for Eleanor and Papa to sing. There was just time to dress for church. I wore my blue serge wool with the lace collar. Carlie insisted on wearing her pink silk party dress with the smocking. "That's a summer dress," I said, but Carlie wouldn't give in.

"It's my *best* dress," she said, and wriggled into it.

When Papa and Eleanor marched in with the choir, Carlie pinched me. Eleanor sang a solo that had lovely words from one of the psalms: "As the hart panteth after the water brooks, so panteth my soul after thee, O God." I knew that a hart was a deer, and I wondered if Eleanor was thinking of the deer she'd once tamed and had to shoot. It didn't look like it, because her face shone like it always did when she sang. I saw Papa watching her, and I pinched Carlie back.

The Thurstons came up to us after church while we were waiting for Eleanor and Papa to leave the choir room. Papa came out first, still buttoning his over-coat. He said to Mrs. Thurston, "Elvira, I wonder if I could impose myself upon you. Would you take in a hungry man for dinner? The girls have invited Eleanor for dinner, and I would only be in the way."

I had to bite my tongue to keep from crying out, but Carlie didn't bite hers. "Papa, you're supposed to be at our dinner. It's for you and Eleanor."

Dr. and Mrs. Thurston looked from Carlie to Papa, who had turned beet red. There was no time to say any-thing more, for Eleanor was coming. Mrs. Thurston said, "Excuse us for just a moment, Edward." She grabbed my hand and Carlie's and led us off. The minute we were far enough away that she wouldn't be heard, Mrs. Thurston said, "Girls, you have put your father and Eleanor in a very difficult position. It is not fair to Eleanor. People will talk."

I remembered how Mrs. Lartner had looked when she saw Papa and Eleanor together at the piano. "Meddling mischief-maker," Papa had said. It was unfair. How could our plan work if they weren't allowed to be together?

Carlie said, "But we want them to get married."

Mrs. Thurston wiped away Carlie's tears with her lace handkerchief.

"That thought must come from them, not from you, and I don't think either Eleanor or your father has any idea of such a thing."

I didn't believe that. I remembered how Papa looked at Eleanor in the choir. All I could think of was how perfect it would be if they got married. But I had to admit that for now we would have to give up our plans for having the two of them together for dinner.

We tried to hide our disappointment as we led Eleanor back home. I sneaked into the dining room to remove the extra setting before she could see it and wonder what had made Papa change his plans. Eleanor exclaimed over the mayonnaise. "I've never tasted better," she said. "Very fancy!" After a bit we were so happy to have her there that we tried to put aside the terrible failure of our plans and make Eleanor's visit pleasant for her.

"I've made friends with the other women attendants," Eleanor said. "We get twenty dollars a month and our room and board. I'll soon be rich. It helps that I can speak German. I long to know their stories, but they are like books you can't open. They seem so miserable, and it makes me so happy when the music helps.

"The attendants live on the fourth floor. We report for duty at seven in the morning, and we're on duty until eight in the evening, but Sunday afternoons like this we have off. They're all really nice girls. None of us has much, so we share. This shawl belongs to one of them."

I was angry with Papa for not being there to admire the shawl that Eleanor had specially worn. After dinner I played piano, and Eleanor and Carlie sang. When it was time for Eleanor to go, Carlie and I walked her back to the asylum. The sky was streaked with purple. There was a sliver of new moon. Snow fell in big soft flakes covering Dr. Thurston's grass and trees and Louis's flower beds. The snow pulled away all the color. Ahead of us was the asylum. With its lighted windows it looked like a great ship on a white ocean.

"I'll tell you a secret," Eleanor said. "There's going to

be a training school for nurses right here, and some of us attendants might get to sign up." Eleanor kissed both of us and disappeared into the asylum, leaving Carlie and me to walk back alone.

The day before, one of Aunt Maude's letters had come. She had asked after each of us and sent along some instructions for Mrs. Luth on how to take care of the fireplaces in winter. When I opened her letters, I felt little puffs of icy air escape. Soon Papa would be back home from the Thurstons'. He would go into his study, close the door, and work on his book. I was sure he liked Eleanor. I was sure I didn't think it just because I wanted it to be true. But he would do nothing about it. Eleanor's and Carlie's hearts were there for everyone to see. Aunt Maude's and Papa's hearts were shut away in their locked gardens. I wasn't sure about my own heart. I was a little afraid to be like Carlie and Eleanor, so quick to love that you might get hurt, but I didn't want to be like Aunt Maude and Papa, so cautious that loving got away from you.

"What can we do now?" Carlie asked, but I had no answer. I had learned that there were times when you just had to do something, like the time I had gone out to the farm to rescue Eleanor. And there were times when you had to let people make up their own minds, like Eleanor had to choose for herself whether to go with her father. I thought about the horses on John's farm, standing patiently, day after day. I wished I could be that patient, but I knew I couldn't. I reached for Carlie's mittened hand and hung on. "We'll think of something," I said.

Author's Note

Hospitals for the mentally ill, or asylums, as they were called in Verna's time, have long been controversial. From early times to the 1800s, the mentally ill were often considered possessed by the devil. They were shut away in cells, where they were treated like animals, sleeping upon beds of straw and chained to walls. People paid to come to asylums and jeer at the patients.

In the 1840s a nurse, Dorothea Dix, led a movement in this country to reform asylums and to treat mental illness as what it is, an illness like any other.

During the years 1870 to 1910, the time of my story, there was a movement across the country to build well-furnished, handsome hospitals where patients could recover through a combination of pleasant surroundings and purposeful work. Frederick Law Olmsted, the landscape architect who created Central Park in New York City, designed the grounds of the Buffalo State Asylum for the Insane in New York.

Not all hospitals for the mentally ill adhered to these high standards. Many hospitals abused patients, resorting to cruel restraints and harsh treatment. In later years there were objections to making patients work, and there were many who believed patients would be better off treated not in large hospitals but near their families, in their own communities, and in small group homes.

In our time new medications have revolutionized the treatment of the mentally ill and have made it possible for many of them to live happy, fulfilling lives.

Although *The Locked Garden* is fiction and all the characters are imagined, my story was inspired by Traverse City State Hospital in Traverse City, Michigan, where the hospital's first superintendent, Dr. James Decker Munson, emphasized the importance of pleasant surroundings in the treatment of the mentally ill. I was also inspired by a book about that hospital, *Angels in the Architecture: A Photographic Elegy to an American Asylum*, by Heidi Johnson.

National Book Award—winning author **GLORIA WHELAN** is the bestselling author of many novels for young readers, including *Homeless Bird*, winner of the National Book Award, *After the Train*, *Parade of Shadows*, and *Listening for Lions*. She lives in northern Michigan. You can visit her online at www.gloriawhelan.com.